DANCING WITH THE DOGS AND OTHER STORIES

ANTHEA SENARATNA

May 2002
November 2006
February 2009

Cover illustration by the author

Published by
Anthea Senaratna

Printed by
Ari Investments Ltd., Nugegoda.
2852410, 2820019

ISBN 955-97754-0-5

Introduction & Acknowledgements

At last, I say to myself, as I put out this set of stories! They've been weighing heavily on me, and I'm relieved they're off now.

Most of the stories are based on anecdotes drawn from real life experiences, so this business about the characters being entire works of fiction is not quite true! Of course they are caricatures of what happens in real life. On the other hand, some of the stories are just stories- made up ones, where the situations and characters are realistic but not real.

There are many people I have to thank for the help and support they gave me in making this book a reality. First of all, of course, is Simon, whose willingness, not only to be featured in some of the stories, but also to read, criticize, encourage and egg me on to write; for his sheer doggedness to ask me every single day this past year "howzthebookhowzthebookhowzthebook?" Thank you Simon for your immense faith and confidence in me. My gratitude to my children Sonali and Dimitri and their respective spouses Dinesh and Sarah, whose constant query of "How's it going?" kept my fingers tapping. I must also thank my sister Lorni, my special friends Kamala and Frank, and all those wonderful people in the English Writers' Workshop (Wadiya Group), who have helped me in so many different ways to put this collection together.

I cannot forget to pay tribute to my 'other' family – my beloved doggies, without whom the title for this book would never have come about. At least I could write about them honestly knowing full well that they will not sue me for defamation. I am also grateful to my ever faithful Kusum, whose help in relieving me of tedious household chores, gives me the time and space to sit down and write.

As the only 'animal' with the ability to laugh, I believe we, humans, should practise this art more often – especially the art of laughing at ourselves. So, I hope these stories will brighten your spirits somewhat, especially in times such as these, when we are besieged by terrorism and violence, and have a definite need to look at the lighter side of life occasionally in order to de-stress ourselves.

Anthea Senaratna

Contents

Chaos at the Circus

The Circus was in a mess. Its arena was splattered with dead bodies of Lions and Tigers. It had turned into quite a big battle. The Lions and the Tigers found it hard to resolve their problems by friendly discussion. The territory, they said, had to be divided properly. The Lions did make an offer, but of course there were so many things that the Tigers didn't like about the deal, they just threw the piece of paper on which the conditions were written, out of the window. They pulled out their guns and grenades and growled at the Lions. The Lions, not to be belittled, also pulled out all the stops as they say, which in this case meant arms and ammunition. Now that rhetoric had failed, they roared down on the Tigers with their rifles and wrath. The war was now in full swing.

There were many many deaths and casualties on both sides. The reports exaggerated or understated the numbers, depending on who was reporting what, so that the lions and tigers who were not in the Circus and wanted nothing more than to get about their business of everyday life, peacefully, never knew the true story.

In addition to this, the Lions began fighting among themselves. Each of them wanted to be a leader; each of them spent a great deal of time describing the faults of the others; they had inquiries and commissions, and the local newspapers which were run by the Clowns, were full of reports on the findings of these investigations. The newspapers also took sides, so one never knew the truth in this case either. The Lions spoke publicly against one another, calling their fellow creatures rogues and robbers and condemning their own kind to the furious fires of hell. They began pummelling each other like prize boxers gone berserk, and it was fashionable to have one's very own gang of thugs to deal with any disagreements they might encounter. They became cleverer and cleverer at making more and more money - those lovely crisp bits of paper that could get them anything they wanted, and get rid of whatever they didn't want. They resorted to using firearms in "teaching the others a lesson", and it became a common occurrence for important and even the not so important Lions to be killed off without so much as blinking an eyelid. The Lions had now acquired a Gun Culture which was something quite alien to their reputation of hospitality and kindness and their awesome two thousand year history which was the pride of their Pride. Colours became a vital issue in their lives. Some of them thought Green was gorgeous, while others felt Blue was better. Still others down the line preferred a spectrum of colours enough to make any rainbow fade in shame. They showed their true colours indeed when they took pot shots at people merely at the drop of a chair, or elephant or whatever. They liked playing games. Prior to the local elections they played "Anything you can do I can do better" and went around in their vans shouting at the top of their voices about how wonderful they were. Then they played the Pasting the Posters game and plastered pictures of themselves on every bare inch of wall space. The whole place was turned into a Rogues Gallery with the posters of faces and skulls and a naked man strung up on a post, glaring out from every wall, pillar and post. They then played the Removing the Posters Game, whereby they sent their gangs to remove posters of their rivals. So you saw one gang of goons busily pasting pictures and another busily tearing them off. They carried out this senseless activity so seriously, it must have been some sort of therapeutic exercise for them.

Meanwhile the Tigers, also a Gun-Toting lot, were pulling out their maps and collecting great hoardes of crisp currency for themselves. They were humming quietly to themselves the "Anything you can do WE can do Better" theme. They also began polishing their guns, collecting more ammunition, laying down land-mines, creating live bombs - all in an effort to defeat the enemy. They were out to get the Lions. The arena was going to be theirs, they claimed. They thought it mighty funny that the Lions should kill each other off - for this was what they, the Tigers were supposed to do, and now it was all being done for them. They just sat on the side lines and watched, greatly amused at the incredible fracas which was taking place among the Leos. Off an on they would gather together and charge growlingly at a bunch of Lions who never knew what hit them. They were so busy hitting each other, that they did not even notice that the Striped Felines had infiltrated their lot.

And so life went on. While the Lions were involved in murdering and marauding their own kind, the Tigers were quietly planning and preparing some dreadful surprise to spring on them. The Tigers were invisibly invading the arena where the Lions were busy killing themselves off. They could make the stripes on their bodies completely disappear and some of them would wear a false mane around their necks to look like the real Lions. They turned themselves into jugglers and trapeze artistes and mingled with the Circus crowd. All the time they practised their skills they were surrounded by the Lions who were now worn out and weary with trying to win their own wishy-washy whims and wants. Before they realized it, the unsuspecting Lions found themselves surrounded by the Tigers who had by now resumed their own identities. The Lions who were in a total state of disarray were too bewildered to do anything constructive to defend themselves, and the Tigers who were bonded by the bands on their bodies and clung close to one another with their cunning and cleverness, had taken the entire arena. They just tossed the beaten bunch of battered lions over the fence.

And so the battle was over; the Lions roamed outside the main arena and were lucky if they got an old bone thrown over to them by the Terrible Tigers. "If only we had stuck together, we could have had this arena all to ourselves" the Lions moaned in regret. But it was too late.

A hundred years later Tiger archaeologists found the skulls and bones of many of the Lions who were killed in these battles. They kept them in their Museums and the schooling Tigers looked at them with interest.

"Long long ago," the Tiger guide intoned, "there were Lions living in this arena. But many of them killed one another and our great Tiger Leaders just threw those who remained over the border and they were too weak and too worn out and could not fight back. They were totally annihilated and this is all we have left of them - their bones."

The little Tigers looked sadly at the bones.

The well formed skulls and handsome body structure suggested they must have been magnificent creatures.

"Were they clever?" asked a little Tiger.

"Oh yes - and artistic and always smiling and friendly -"

"Such a pity they couldn't get on with each oither."

"Such a downright shame!"

Dancing with the Dogs!

"Write about the dogs." my family pleaded with me.

"Yes, yes - do write about us!" my canine family echoed the human pleas, jumping all over me, begging me to put their names in print.

So here I am, all set to write about my dogs. I have had so many dogs in my life that it is hard to know where I should begin. To begin at the beginning will surely end up with several volumes of doggie stories. So, for the moment I suppose I should concentrate on our doggie family who live with us at the moment.

Firstly, I have to confess that we are still not sure who owns whom. I mean do we own the dogs or do they own us? It is a controversial point - perhaps the reader will be able to reach some reasonable conclusion, if he is sane enough to do so at the end of this story.

We live in a small compact three bedroomed house. So do the dogs. There are seven human beings and five dogs under the same roof. From their point of view, they have a father - Simon, mother - me of course, someone to cook for them - Kusum, playmates - Sonali, Dimitri and Kumara (Kusum's son). Our driver is there to take them around in the car when Simon is busy. From our point of view, they are our little babas who play with us and greet us with unmitigated joy at whatever ungodly time we get back home. Their affection for us is unbelievable. They are our constant companions when we are at home, and where we are, they are.

We bought Jasper when he was a six week old puppy, from a strange large lady, who wept copiously when we took him away. We were looking for a golden male cocker spaniel and there he was, the only one of that colour in a litter of six full black cockers. We fell in love with him at once. When I had to pay for him, the owner immediately burst into tears and her aged mother who was there grabbed her in her arms, and said "There there" to her, and made signs at me to put the cash on the table and beat it fast. My driver hearing all the commotion came inside wondering whether I was involved in some fracas with the owner. I did what I had to do - put the money on the table and left pronto - with the golden bundle of fur squealing in my arms. It was a relief to get into the car and be on our way home.

Then after almost a year we got Jenna. We felt that Jasper needed a companion. In actual fact, we just wanted another dog. But being human beings we felt we had to have some logical reason for our action, so we cooked up this story about Jasper wanting a friend. At a certain age and stage Jenna produced litters of incredibly beautiful little cocker spaniels. From the first batch, we were compelled to keep Jessica and Julie as they fell prey to a deadly doggie disease and had to be treated over a period of time. By the time they were completely cured they were too old to be given away. From a later litter we kept Jody who was the only black and white pup in the multi-coloured selection which Jenna had produced. She was too beautiful to leave us so we did the next best thing - we kept her.

So now we had the five Js. They were all different colours and made an interesting picture, especially when they were together. Jasper is brown with golden ears, white chest and a snout of white with brown freckles. Jenna is jet black. Jessica is plain brown. Julie is brown with lighter ears, and Jody is white with black ears and head and black patches on her body. People gasped in disbelief when they asked us how many dogs we had, and we told them nothing but the truth. After the shock wore off they would continue to give us strange looks- wondering at our insanity.

Jasper, who was a most delightful puppy, has grown up to be a handsome dog. His colour combination together with his smiling eyes and face make him very appealing. But somehow, he acquired some strange quirks along the way. He developed an uncanny liking or dislike - depending from which angle you look at it - for feet. For feet that belonged to human beings, that is. He bites all the human feet he comes across, regardless to whom they are attached. In this unusual hobby of his, he has bitten everyone in the house, and many unfortunate persons who happened to cross his path, or rather his jaws. When Jenna came into heat, the time when female canines become all sultry and seductive and lure the male of the species into exciting adventures, she pranced around the house executing her entire dance repertoire with Jasper following closely on her heels - looking rather foolish in his wild frenzy to keep up with her. While doing this, he snapped at all the unwitting and unfortunate feet that happened to be in his way. One evening Simon was bitten twice on his feet within a period of about fifteen minutes. We understood that Jasper was trying to get into the Guiness Book of Records - for the most number of bites in the shortest space of time, and had to forgive him of course. When he has to be bathed or taken to the vet, I have to work out a different strategy each time. The last time I took him to the vet's he refused to get off the car when we stopped outside Dr.Ching's. I tried coaxing him and called him all the affectionate names I could think of, but with no avail. I tried forcing him to get down and when he growled I knew I had to change tactics. So I got back into the car, and we drove along a few yards, stopped at some other house whereupon he very gladly got off the car. Then I walked him to the vet's. Fortunately for me, he was too bewildered to protest when he found himself there.

Jenna has grown up to be a very sweet natured and pretty dog and is blessed with a high degree of intelligence. Her olfactory senses can not only detect a million things dogs usually sniff out, but also she can smell Love Cake, Coconut Rock, cheese and grapes a mile away. All she needs is a pair of dark glasses and a glass of wine and she would be set to relax on the Riviera. Jenna thinks (as the others do too) that everything in the house belongs to her - especially our bedroom and bathroom. Often one would find her fast asleep on the bed looking as though this was indeed her very own bed. She definitely believes that the bathmats in the bathroom are meant for her to roll around on; after all who would put pieces of towelling on the floor for any other purpose? So the bathmats are always tossed in some corner of the bathroom and never where they should be. Jenna had all her litters in our bedroom. I had to place a box of the appropriate size and she would get into it for days before the pups were due. Somehow her doggie instinct told her that this was to be the delivery room, or to use "canine" language, the whelping box. When the crucial moment arrived, either Simon or I had to stay by her side until the last pup was born. Often this took several hours and we had to pet her and console her and tell her what a wonderful little doggie she was, right through the birth process of the entire litter! Simon had his special language for her and he would tell her what a bingle bongle girl she was and there it was - another little coochie poochie puppy! After the entire litter was out, we all had a rest, Jenna and the two of us. The pups were of course too small to bother about anything. She was always the perfect mother, caring over them all the time. In fact she groomed them so much that sometimes their fur would get matted together and had to be cleaned carefully. Even after the pups were old enough to be put into a "play-pen" when they were three to four weeks old, she would stay in with them and fuss over them no end.

Jenna is Simon's shadow. She has taken him over completely. If you see her, you know Simon is not far behind. Even when she eats Simon has to stand by her. Why, just the other day a friend decided to visit us. As she peeped over our rear gate, she spied Simon in the kennel (we have kennels with high roofs so that we could get inside and clean them easily).

Simon was actually standing there reading a book while Jenna was having her lunch. Of course my friend did not see Jenna - all she saw was Simon reading a book inside the dog kennel.

"My uncle!" she exclaimed, "what are you doing inside the dog's kennel!"

"I'm waiting for Jenna to finish her lunch." Simon replied, rather peeved at having to leave his book even for a second.

"Oh," said my friend, "I thought of coming and visiting all of you."

"No no - don't come now - come after Jenna finishes her lunch."

"Ah - then I'll come some other time." she must have been peeved too - after all she could not see this dog having her lunch - and anyway what was Simon doing there reading a book? Maybe she thought I had punished him?

Later on when I met her, she said to me "My aunty, you'll have a big problem no - and I saw uncle the other day in the dog cage - reading a book." She said this questioningly - the unsolved mystery in her mind! Nothing I said could convince her of the real situation.

Jody has turned into a beautiful dog with silky black ears and a face so expressive you could actually read her thoughts. She too has joined Jenna in tagging along behind Simon. Their entire life revolves around him. When he is at home on a holiday, they know it is a holiday. They know from his shorts and slippers that today is a fun day - that he will not be going to dull places such as the office. They become so glued to him that they refuse to leave him even for a second.   The afternoons are their favourite time of the day. It is the time during which they are taken for a drive. When Simon rests after lunch, Jenna sleeps at the foot of the bed, and Jody on the floor beside him. He cannot even blink twice without making them sit up and take notice. As soon as he gets up they are up as well. Excited to a fever pitch they run around barking wildly. Recently, Julie has also taken to going out with them for their drives. So they all dash screeching to the car and what a scramble it is to get inside. Finally Simon gets in and they are off on their drive. It is a sight to behold! There is Simon, concentrating one hundred percent on his driving. Jenna is seated next to him on the front seat observing the world go by. Jody is seated on the gear stick. She looks through the front windscreen and when she spots a dog, which is about once every minute - she barks ferociously. Then she jumps onto the back seat, puts her paws up and peers through the rear window and continues to bark - "I'll kill you!" she says! During all this hullabaloo, Julie is lying on the floor at the back giving out high pitched squeaky shrieks all the time. Through this cacophony they are taken to exciting and adventurous places like the Bewitched Junction at Kirillaponne, the Enchanted Roundabout at Narahenpita and even sometimes to the Magic Land of Nugegoda! They are back within fifteen or twenty minutes, thoroughly exhausted and happy beyond words, panting and wagging their little tails till they almost drop off. Every night after our dinner the dogs wait to be taken out for a run on the road just outside our house. What this means is that the dogs run and Simon just stands, supervising. As soon as Simon gets up from the table, they are all lined up and ready near the front door - ready to go out! Jenna barks and gets them all together and they just dash out wildly when the gate is opened. Jasper keeps away from the girls and has to be called and coaxed to come out with them.

Our dogs are the most untrained specimens ever. They have voted for democracy and as a result indulge in freedom of barks, freedom of movement and in fact freedom in everything. A friend from a farm in Australia was honestly surprised to find that our dogs did not work for their keep. The dogs on her farm, she said, had to work pretty hard and in all kinds of inclement weather too, right throughout the year, and it was only when they were old or had some physical disability and were unable to cope with working, were they permitted to retire. Our dogs were on holiday from the day they were born.

Simon is great at giving them commands. In fact when visitors are present Simon pretends that the dogs are graduates of the Police Dog Training Academy and will obey any command given to them. So there he is saying "Sit" and "Come here" in that correct tone of voice and all the dogs do is jump on him and bark. In fact, a house guest remarked that he found our dogs "delightfully disobedient at all Simon's futile attempts to order them around!" Once when Jody was lying on the bed enjoying the breeze of the fan on her belly and Simon was lying on the (same) bed reading, I told him to get her off the bed, because there was no room for me there. He leaned over to her and said very gently, "Jody, she says to get off the bed." The "she" in this instance being me of course. Jody's response was a big wag and a giggle. Then Simon pointed to the floor and said "You must get down there" at which Jody also leaned over with him and they both took a good look at the floor for about a minute, and then they both got back on to the bed. "She is not getting off" said Simon in a most uninterested tone, and went back to his book.

Jody has her special games with Simon. After we have dinner and the dogs have gone on their little run, it is time for Jody to play "Pillow." In her language we call it "Pilly" - don't ask me why, perhaps because it rhymes with silly. Jody runs to our room where I have some special pillows (complete with doggie printed covers) for any dog who wants a pillow for the night. She pulls them down from the stand on which they are kept and jumps on to the bed with them. Simon has to growl at her and pretend to rough her up a bit and she growls in return. Then he takes the pillow or the pilly and throws it onto the floor whereupon Jody leaps onto it, and growling, takes it back with her onto the bed. This goes on over and over again and when we are all exhausted - although I must admit we tire more easily than Jody does, the game is over. Simon has so many conversations with the dogs, that the other day a friend questioned - "Is he talking to himself or to the dogs?" She peeped into the room and said to herself, "Ah yes, he's chatting to Jody."

Julie is a dinky little light brown cocker spaniel with a beautiful face and long golden ears. She can wag her tail and her rear with the expertise of a Hawaiian dancer. Like King Arthur searched for the Holy Grail, Julie searches for her Mommy. Mommy, of course, is me. She follows me everywhere. When I am in the bathroom, she comes in and sleeps on the bath mat. Her favourite time is after lunch when she waits to have a nap with me. She jumps onto the bed and snuggles right next to me with her head buried in my pillow. She is the kind of dog that could be a Rapunzel - with her long golden hair. Perhaps one of these days some doggie will see her at the upstair window and call out to her to "let down her hair" - I guess her reply would be "If you want me, my Mommy comes too."

Jessica was never intended to be a dog. She looks more like Winnie the Pooh. Her physical proportions and facial expressions are definitely Pooh Bear. Sadly, Jessica is now blind in both her eyes. But this does not deter her from all the fun and antics she has been used to in the past. Although she has slowed down considerably, she manages to get around quite well. She still has a good bark at a crow or a cat or another dog. She is confident in her knowledge that we are always there to care for her. She is a dog of peculiar noises. When she scratches her ears she makes one noise, and when she scratches her leg it is another kind of whine. When she is nervous, like at the vets, or when she is being bathed, she makes all sorts of strange squeaky blurps.

Kusum loves the dogs with an unquestionable affection. Even Jasper who has bitten her more than once is treated with the utmost loving tender care. They adore her as much as she loves them. To me the most entertaining time of day is to witness them being given their mid-day meal. They eat only once a day and have five separate cages as their dining quarters. First Kusum calls Jasper, as he has to be got out of the way before the others are fed. So it goes- "Jaspie boy, Jaspie boy, go into your cage like a good doggie." When it suits him, Jasper just goes into his cage but more often than not he takes his own time about it. So he just lies down and folds his paws and looks bored. You'd expect him to pull out a cigarette and puff on it.

Kusum then goes "There Jaspie, good Jasper boy, go soon and eat otherwise the crow will take your food away!"

Jasper is now examining his paws and claws. Kusum tries again, "Come Jaspie boy, good boy, Jaspie is MY good boy. He is going to eat all his lunch now!"

Jasper just looks at Kusum. What is wrong with this woman, he wonders. Jaspie boy, Jaspie boy - can't she do something else instead of just saying Jaspie boy Jaspie boy? He shuts his eyes and pretends to sleep. Kusum by now has snapped. She shrieks, "Jasper go into your cage at once, otherwise I'll just throw your lunch into the dustbin and you can starve. I shan't cook for you tomorrow - or ever again, you just wait and see. Bad dog!"

She storms back into the house to get the other dogs their food. A crow is perched on the door of his cage eyeing his food greedily. Jasper watches the crow. He is perturbed. He might well lose his entire meal to this measly black thing with wings. He gets up and rushes at the crow growling and barking as if he is warding off a herd of elephants. The crow makes a quick getaway. Jasper goes into his cage and begins to eat. Kusum comes out of the house and sees this.

"Ha! At last you have decided to eat. Good thing before the crow ate it up." She closes the door to his cage firmly so that he cannot get out. "Aney Jasper boy, my silly little patiya. Gooood little patiya." Jasper is engrossed in his meal and pays no attention to her.

Jessica and Jody love their food. Jody just skips and barks and is oh in such a joyous state when she gets the aroma of the meat and all the good things that Kusum has so lovingly cooked for her. In fact Jody makes all sorts of silly noises which Kusum explains to me - she is asking for her lunch. So Kusum says to her. "My Sudu Baba, do you want your lunch?" Jody barks and wags her tail and runs to her cage! Jessie and Jody guzzle down their food just like dogs are supposed to. Jenna and Julie are another matter altogether. Kusum goes "Jenna, are you going to eat now or will you eat later?" Jenna just looks at her and decides she could eat later. "Ah Jenna, where's my Kalu Amma, where's this Jenna girl?" Jenna looks at her in total disbelief. Here she is in front of Kusum and she is asking where she is. Maybe her eyes are playing up. In any case Jenna wants to wait until Simon turns up for lunch, then she will decide when she will eat

Kusum comes to Julie, who is sitting curled up at my feet. "Joolie, Joolie where is my Joolie girl? Joola, Joola come Joola and eat." Shades of Rapunzel Rapunzel where are you Rapunzel! Julie just looks up at Kusum. "Ah that means that she will eat later - at three o'clock." Kusum says to me. If ever anyone needs a dog psychiatrist I could always recommend Kusum. At precisely one minute to three, Kusum tackles Julie about eating her lunch. "Come Joola come Joola and eat your lunch." Julie now runs to her cage wagging her stubby little tail with all her might. She sits by her plate and looks dolefully at the contents. What's this, she thinks. I thought it was going to be roast chicken and macaroni. Drat! it's the same old boiled mush.

"Come Julie, eat your lunch like a good doggie." coaxes Kusum with infinite patience. She sits down beside Julie. "Now Joola," she says, stroking her head and long silky ears, "You had better eat soon, otherwise Whiskers will come and eat it all up." Then up into the unknown, "Whiskers, Whisky, come and eat Joola's food, come Whiskers." Whiskers was our beloved cat who passed on to some higher feline plane many years ago. So Julie is quite puzzled. She does not want to allow Whiskers to come from wherever she was to eat up her lunch. Better for her to start eating it up soon before Whiskers pounces on it! Julie eats with delicate little nibbles, and soon she licks the bowl clean. So much for Whisker's chances. She comes running out of her cage wagging her tail joyfully. She leaps on me shaking in ecstasy. "Missie, ask her whether she has had her lunch," Kusum tells me. So I say "Julie did you have your lunch?" She smacks her lips in acknowledgement, and squeals in delight.

The sound of our doorbell excites the dogs no end. I often wonder whether there is some electronic device within them that causes such pandemonium when some unfortunate person places a finger on the doorbell. The poor soul on the other side of the gate gets the distinct impression that a pack of wolves is about to descend on him. To hear them barking and growling gives the visitor the feeling that he is entering not into the house of a friend, but into a den of wild animals. Jenna has recently taken lessons in opera singing and greets Simon whenever he comes in with a piercing yodel of howls, encouraging the others to join in - right until he walks into the house whereupon they stop their wails and leap on him accompanied by a rhapsody of barks.

It is night time in the Senaratna household. The dogs have had their little run on the road, and Jody has had a surfeit of her game of "Pillies." It is now time to go to bed. Jenna has her set place which is under Simon's bed. Julie runs along to Kusum's room to sleep on the chair there. In the middle of the night she visits our room. She passes my side of the bed and goes all the way round to Simon's side. Then she squeals in staccato bursts, until he wakes up -(anyone is compelled to wake up with the constant high pitched squeaks)- and he gets up and brings her over to my side! He thinks she is testing his true love for her - I think she is just nuts! Jessica also sleeps in Kusum's room. Jody more often than not leaps onto our bed in the middle of the night to announce that she has decided to sleep with us. She jumps right on to Simon and licks his face and draws his attention with her paw, to say "Hi, I'm here." Regardless of what time it is, Simon never never gets impatient with her. He always responds with "Yes, yes you are a good little girl." Then she turns around and sleeps at his feet. Jasper takes frequent walks in the night. He walks from Kusum's room to our room and then back again. He too often announces his presence by licking my face or my hand, and sometimes he even springs on the bed to sleep at my feet. I must say I do get into a cold sweat when I feel a furry creature at my feet, and discover that it is none other than the Foot Biter himself! I have installed a "doggie door" on the rear door. Through this, the dogs can leave and return on their own, without needing anyone to open and close the door for them. It is the most convenient contraption we have got, and serves its purpose perfectly. So we hear the sound of the door flapping up and down as they go in and out. They are always ready to bark at the mice and the bandicoots who scuttle around the garden at night, but on two occasions when burglars prowled outside the house the Guardians of the

House were discovered on their backs, fast asleep and snoring. I well recall once when there were some strange noises from outside, Jody promptly leapt on our bed and barked and nudged me with her paw - "Get up and go have a look," she seemed to say, while I, bleary eyed, walked around flashing a torch, she curled up and went to sleep on the bed. So much for them being Guard Dogs.

When morning comes they are all there to greet us. Jenna knows it is the time for her to roll on the bath mats. Jasper comes in smiling and wants to be petted. Jessica walks into our room to say "Hello." Jody does not have to move at all as she is already on the bed, so she just looks up and wags her tail. Julie sleeps late. She stumbles in sleepily and looks at me through half closed eyes, wagging her little tail very slowly. The time has come once again for the Senaratna household - and the J Five, to face the challenges of yet another day.

Searching for Brahms

Simon and I were having a drink together.

"Let's drink a toast to Brahms," he said.

"Brahms - why Brahms?" I asked.

"Why - don't you remember, it's one year since I went searching for Brahms - during the power cut last year?"

Then I remembered. Last year this time.

The year is 1996.

The power cuts seem to be going on forever. They began in the middle of March and this is now the middle of June and we are still having power cuts during the day. Two hours in the morning, two at mid-day, and one and a half in the evening. The times rotate in the different areas so we have to keep a close watch on the clocks in order not to get caught to one of these dreadful dark currentless periods without warning. All our time is spent clock watching - how long more for the power to be cut and how long more for the power to come on. From a nation who normally didn't care two hoots about time, we have now been turned into fiendish clock watchers, and those little hands which mattered not a jot to us have taken on a life and death countenance.

Going out during the power cuts is more than just an outing: it is a challenge to one's character, a test to one's sanity - in fact it is an Odyssey - full of adventure. Try going to one of Colombo's famous shopping malls. The most important items you should remember to take are your torch and a little oxygen cylinder. It is so dark and stifling inside the mall, the shop assistants gasp the prices at you and faint right there at your feet. So the place is strewn with bodies, which you may well trip over as you can't see beyond your nose, remember. Of course when the power comes on - they all revive like the princess who slept until the prince found her. With the magic kiss of electricity they are all brought back to life, instantly!

Inside the shops is yet another story. Most places are so dark it's like visiting the catacombs in Rome! Either take a torch with you or if you want both hands free wear one of those miner's lights on your head. I must say that other shoppers looked strangely at me when I donned the latter - but who cares? In the dark no one could see my face - it was when I came out of the building into the streaming, screaming sunlight that I got these weird looks. Strange.

Simon wanted to buy a CD. The CD shop was in a state of twilight - it had some strange source of energy that gave it an ethereal glow. Through the pale shadows Simon groped his way carefully until he could dimly visualise the square CD containers smiling at him.

"I'm looking for Brahms" said Simon.

"Gone for lunch" replied the shop assistant nonchalantly picking his finger nails.

Simon looked non plussed. " Lunch? Must have gone a long time ago!"

The shop assistant gave him that no nonsense look.

"No just went - will come back soon." he replied, stretching his fingers before him, and admiring them.

Simon's eyes were by now accustomed to the dim atmosphere - he decided to ignore the equally dim assistant and get Brahms himself.

He peered at the CDs nearest to him. "Hmm - these are all Ms - maybe the Bs are up there?" he said looking up the rack.

"Ems and bees? What bees?" the assistant sounded shocked.

"Can you get me those CDs up there -" Simon said in an exasperated tone, as he pointed to the CDs stuck on a shelf ten feet high.

"You must get on stool to get that" said the shop assistant.

"I'm not getting on any stool in the dark - you get it for me." Simon said curtly.

"Aiyo - simple" said the assistant, blowing away the last bit of grub from his nails, and wiping his fingers on his trousers. He stepped on the stool and reached up. A moment later he came crashing down and brought a dozen CDs with him - flying all over the place.

There were shouts of alarm from the dark corners of the shop.

Simon was surprised when he was showered with CDs falling all over him and held up his arms to protect himself. When he regained his composure he discovered that by sheer coincidence or good luck or what-have-you - he actually had the CD he wanted. Brahms in his arms!

The shop assistant picked himself up looking rather stunned and dishevelled. He cleared himself of the CDs which had landed on him and seemed quite chagrined at the unusual turn of events.

"Guess what? "Simon said to the assistant jauntily, "I've got Brahms!" He held the CD close to his chest as if it might disappear into the dim depths of the shop.

The shop assistant paid no attention to his delight. He was nursing a few minor bruises he had encountered in his recent stool climbing effort. He wrote out the bill, silently, with a sullen look on his face.

Simon wavered out of the darkness into the light of the outer world, smiling happily, armed with Brahms and his Third Symphony intact!

The power cut has brought on other problems. I'm going to a party and poof - the lights go off - it's the power cut! So I dress in the dark. I light some candles but after I nearly set fire to my wardrobe, I decided a torch would be safer. So torch in hand I peer into the darkness of my wardrobe. The light gets dimmer - the batteries are down. Damn! But not to worry, I know my clothes so it should be easy. All those clothes hanging up look black - so I just feel around and take something out. It's bound to be alright. I applied my makeup by the light of a flickering candle. I end up at the party looking like I have been appointed the chief clown in some circus! I am wearing my brown trouser with the blue and red blouse - not the black trouser with the pink and black blouse I wanted to wear! And my shoes are green! People are gazing at me in a strange kind of manner. Simon is looking like a thundercloud just about to burst.

"You've got lipstick all over your face!" he hisses into my ear.

I just smile as though he is whispering sweet nothings, and make a bee line for the Ladies.

I see some strange woman looking at me. Lipstick daubed outside her lips and eyeliner making her look like those Pandas the Chinese keep boasting about. I gasp in shock and to my surprise she gasps too. Suddenly it hits me. I am looking at me!

During the power cuts the inside of my house looks and feels like the depths of some dark dungeon. We keep all the doors and windows open to catch what little light and breeze we can, so that we are able to grope our way around the house without meeting with too many accidents. I have run out of candles - the most rare and precious commodity today. So I eat in the dark - it is an interesting exercise to taste what you cannot see. It will make my taste buds sharper, they say. Suddenly I find myself chewing stubbornly on something, and discover to my horror that it is the cloth napkin which was neatly folded on my side plate!

Someone knocks at the gate and I shout "It's not locked – come right in." My neighbour Padma has promised to visit me, and now that my sense of hearing is more acute, I am certain I recognise her footsteps.

"Ah come in Padma!" I say, happy to have company to cheer me up.

Silence.

Then suddenly someone grabs me, and before I can even squeak I am gagged and trussed up. To my great horror I realise that I have let in a burglar on his late evening rounds. He flashes a torch up and down and I see him snatching my new clock plus the two bronze horses from the side table in the sitting room. He puts these into a large plastic bag he has brought with him.

A knock on the gate sends him scurrying out of the back door. This must be Padma, but try as I might, I cannot call out to her. Almost half an hour later I hear the garage open and the sound of the car. It's Simon. He flashes a torch and is quite surprised to find me in this position.

"Why are you torturing yourself - you knew I was getting late." he scoffs.

And so life goes on. I languish during the power cuts - waiting eternally for the lights to come back; waiting for the darkness to lift. Waiting for the fans to play some cool breeze upon my sweaty brow. Waiting to check my email, waiting to get on with my stories - waiting for life to get back into its normal stride. Waiting to get my sanity back.

Waiting.

We clink our glasses. "Here's to electricity - I hope we never have those dreadful cuts again." I say.

"Here's to Brahms!" says Simon.

The magic of Brahms' Third Symphony fills the air.

Getting Ready for New Year

The New Year will soon be here. Kusum has been preparing for this event for the past so many months. When the last new year was over - she started talking about this year's avuruddu celebrations.

She said "My, now again next year it will be new year!" with such eager anticipation, one would have thought it was just around the corner. But it was twelve whole months away. Three hundred and sixty five days. And yet, to her, time had leapt forwards and catapulted the much awaited festival to the immediate future!

About a month ago, the price of eggs at the nearby kade escalated. I protested at this unreasonable increase.

"That is because of the New Year" explained Kusum to me.

"But that's a month away!" I replied.

"Yes - but from now itself everything will go up in price. I must buy some flour and keep to take home before that also goes up in price. Ah - and I must buy some parippu and some miris karal also." Kusum intoned.

I met the kade mudalali. "What is this, you are raising the price of everything because of the New Year - that is almost a month away?" I questioned.

"The prices are going up a little bit now - ha! when the new year is close, they will go up even more." he replied haughtily.

"Aney, I have to buy so many things this time for the home people," Kusum complained, I don't know how I'm going to carry them back in the bus from Nugegoda." She looked at me.

I just listened non committal.

"Missi don't like to go to Nugegoda to see the badus on the pavements? They have shoke badu missi – you will really like them," she continued, not looking up from stirring the curry on the cooker.

Suddenly something happened inside me. Snap, crack, burst- my longing to roam the pavements of Nugegoda couldn't be suppressed any longer; I succumbed to my great yearning and before I could blink, agreed to take her along in the car with me.

The traffic is horrendous. Cars and vans follow each other bumper to bumper. Enormous pickups try to cut their way into the line of traffic. Motor cyclists and push cyclists wind their way in between the larger vehicles and the ubiquitous three wheelers could be spotted, looking like outsize beetles squeezing themselves through invisible gaps in the horde of vehicles. Horns blare with deafening indifference and irate drivers yell insults at one another. No one will give way, so there is a permanent traffic jam. Stray dogs make their way through all this confusion, hoping to pick up some tasty tit-bit from the dustbins and open garbage heaps. The relentless cacophony and the crush of humanity is overwhelming.

We park on a side road as all the parking spaces are full and walk along the pavements looking at this and that. We keep reminding ourselves to hold tightly onto our bags and purses which are being eyed by dozens of camouflaged pickpockets who wait for opportunities like these, when crowds of people jostling against one another make picking a handbag a simple job for them.

The pavements at Nugegoda are unbelievable. It looks like an entire department store has been ransacked and spread out on the streets! Materials by the bale, of every hue, pattern and texture are strewn on plastic cloths. Readymade clothes are piled in large stacks. Makeshift lines are strung across whatever is available, lamp-posts, sides of wooden constructions, poles holding road signs - and blouses and skirts and men's shirts are hung in display. The more expensive ones are enclosed in transparent polythene to protect them from the dust. There are shorts in various colours and sizes; children's caps and clothes; baubles of every kind; underwear for ladies and gents; bags ranging from small to extra large; belts for waists of all dimensions. Then there are the ceramic items - an entire dinner set can be bought piece by piece! Glassware by the dozen; stainless steel and aluminium items pour over each other, and a whole factory of plastic products have been distributed on the pavements. There is a mass of humanity weaving in and out, looking, touching, picking up and examining the multifarious items before making a purchase. The vendors are shouting each other down, trying to make a quick sale over their neighbour, calling out that their goods are the best and the cheapest. There is not an inch of space in between the stalls. Pedestrians have to walk looking down so as not to step on some precious commodity filling up the space on the pavement, and also to avoid falling into some rut or hole in the road. Some of the vendors walk around trying to sell their wares. A man had some skirts hung over his forearm, and one stuck on his head held down firmly with a cap looking like a makeshift nun! Clinching a sale has become the most serious business of the day

Kusum buys materials and blouses and cups and plates and a saucepan and two bedspreads, some towels, plus a set of six glasses. I help her to carry some of her treasure back to the car. I just amble along, mesmerised by the great glut of goodies strewn all over and too overwhelmed to take a decision on purchasing anything.

Kusum has found a friend close by who sews garments. She keeps rushing across at odd intervals and reappears with multi coloured skirts, silk blouses and flowery nightdresses - all for the people at home. Every free moment is devoted to getting something for the "home people." She has bought several bottles of cordial and jam.

"How are you going to carry all these home?" I asked.

"Why, in my bag." she replied making me feel absolutely silly. She paused. "Ah Missi, my bag tore last time I came in the bus, now I don't have a bag." she said, looking at me with a clear hint in her eyes.

So now I give her a bag. I don't know whether it will contain all the paraphernalia she has gathered to take with her.

At long last it is Wednesday, the day for her to go home. She gets up earlier than usual, because, she tells me, that this time she wants to leave really early. Her bed is a mass of garments and packets and bottles. She is busy packing them into her bag. She folds the garments into minute squares so that when she gets to her destination they would look like little crushed up balls of nothing. She comes rushing out of the room.

" Aiyo, I forgot to get a cake to take home. Can't go home without a cake no! Otherwise Nangi will say that I am always coming with nothing in the hand." So she dashes out to look for a cake. Half an hour later she arrives laden with parcels.

"What's all this?" I gasp.

"Why? I thought better to buy some sugar also and some packets of that nice Soya meat."

She collapses exhausted on the bed.

I next see her in the kitchen preparing something for breakfast.

"Why don't you get ready ," I suggest, "I will do the breakfast."

"No no - I will get the breakfast. Sin aney - loku baby has to go to work also." and she bustles around. Her tone implies that I have made a slave of my daughter, sending her out to earn her keep.

"Yes aney I am going home today - I will come back really soon. Can't stay long because I have to do all the work when I go. Then I get a headache. Have to draw water from the well also. Then I get a backache. Real nuisance." While she is saying all this to her friend across the road, her enthusiasm to go becomes clearly diminished. Half an hour later she is still pottering around the kitchen. It is now past nine o'clock.

"Why aren't you going?" I say. I sound like a veteran nagger. "I'm going in a little while, first I must eat no." she says this as if I have prevented her from having her breakfast. Then she sits down with her plate and eats; the radio is on and she is intent on how many terrorists the army has killed. She gives me the latest information.

Nine thirty.

I am tired of seeing her getting ready for so long.

"Why don't you get dressed?" I ask gently this time, so as not to sound offensive.

"Yes -but first I must bathe no!" she sounds clearly annoyed at my constant interruptions.

Half an hour later she emerges from her room in a pink patterned sari.

"See Missi how is this sari?"

"Oh, you look very nice." I reply, hoping that at least now she will start moving.

"Only thing, this jacket is too tight." she grumbles. "I think I will wear the green sari."

The green sari is put on, the jacket fits.

She is combing her hair and patting powder onto her face; daubing some exotic smelling perfume all over herself.

"Aney, Missi set my watch for me." This is always the last request she makes. She cannot read the time but she always wears the watch I gave her.

"All the people in my gama like my watch," she says proudly, "the people in the bus also look at it."

Ten minutes past ten o'clock.

The three wheeler comes to take her to the bus stand.

At last she is ready. She tucks her "porse" as she calls it, with her money, into her blouse. "Nobody can get it now." she says, with a devilish look in her eyes.

She climbs into the vehicle, and her son piles the boxes and bags at her feet and on her lap. You can hardly see her face. It peeps over a bag full of something. Her son gets in with the last heavy box. The three wheeler groans under its elephantine load. We wave to each other and off she goes. She is shouting a muffled "Ta - ta" to our five dogs, who look downcast to see her leave.

She will be back in a week, laden once more. This time it will be with papaws and avocados and bananas from the garden. Jak fruit and seeds in another parcel. The special kalu dhodol her mother has made. And plenty of kavum and kokis - all made at home.

Then she will have another three hundred and sixty five days to look forward to the next New Year!

The Last Ride

The suburb of Saranawila housed a quiet rustic neighbourhood. The shrubs and trees harboured families of birds and butterflies and squirrels and katussas and many other little creatures. Several small cottages stood side by side and the occupants were caring and friendly in a way that defied modern attitudes where no one cared a hoot about who lived next door.

In one of these quaint houses lived Maud Mendelson. Nobody, not even she herself, knew what her age was. One day she was seventy, and a week later she was eighty four. She lived alone. But this did not mean she was lonely. Her neighbours were constantly dropping in on her to see how she was. She also had two nieces who came several times a week with food and other supplies. On one side of her lived two sisters. On the other side lived Amila with her husband and grown-up son. Amila was a schoolteacher and travelled to work early each morning and returned only at mid afternoon when the sun was at its highest.

Every morning on her way to school, Amila saw Maud sitting out on her little verandah. Sometimes she would be reading the newspapers, but sometimes, like today, she was just sitting. Amila waved to her and she waved back. Maud's passion was her plants and she had Gunapala come in every week to attend to the garden.

It was Thursday morning. Mangala and Mihiri, the sisters, were both at home busy with their own work. At about ten o'clock, Gunapala came running in to say that Maud had fallen in her kitchen. Mangala and Mihiri dropped everything and rushed next door. Old Maud was sprawled on the floor. They managed to lift her up - but she was moaning and groaning and it was clear that she needed medical help. So with Gunapala's assistance, they carried her into their car and decided to take her directly to the big Hospital in the City. They left Gunapala in charge of the house. Mihiri sat with Maud in the back seat, while Mangala grabbed the wheel and slammed down hard on the accelerator of her worn out '89 model Lancer, all the way to the hospital.

By now Old Maud looked like she was in a coma. She was just slumped in her seat and seemed quite lifeless. A lady Doctor at the Admissions Desk at the Hospital examined her and looked up solemnly.

"Aiyo Miss, this lady is dead no Miss." she intoned.

"Dead?" the sisters cried. They could hardly believe what they heard.

"Better take her back Miss, otherwise if we take a patient who's dead, there will be a police inquiry and big fuss. Don't you know - there'll be a lot of trouble. So better for you to take her back."

An attendant wheeled the chair back to the car. Mangala and Mihiri were utterly bewildered. They placed Maud on the rear seat and Mihiri climbed in with her. Mihiri had to hold on to Maud as she was falling all over. Mangala, whose hands were now trembling, drove through the heavy traffic, mumbling incoherently.

"Nangi now what are we to do?" she asked. "Where are we to take the body?"

"Where - why to her home of course" snapped Mihiri - "otherwise where?"

Security checkpoints were everywhere in the City. In a nightmarish daze Mangala brought the car to a halt when the Military guard put up his hand, signalling her to stop. "Hide her" she hissed to her sister at the back. Mihiri quickly put Maud down flat, the old lady's head on her lap. She covered the body with a newspaper which was thrown on the back seat. The security guard walked to the car and Mangala put the shutter down.

"ID card Miss" he said hand outstretched. He peered into the car.

"What is that?" he asked staring at the spread out newspaper on the back seat.

Mihiri said quickly, "Aiyo officer, we are taking this very sick lady to the doctor!" She quickly took the newspaper and started fanning Old Maud. The guard eyed her furtively. He stared at the old lady, amazed at the furious pace at which Mihiri was fanning her. Then after leaning into the car and breathing into Mihiri's face, he waved his hand signalling them to move on. Mangala could hardly switch on the ignition, her fingers shook so much.

"Aiyo I don't know what to do" Mangala prattled on, "I can't drive with this corpse in the back seat!"

"You are only driving, sitting in the front. Here I have to hold onto this - this - this body in the back seat - and you are grumbling so much. Fine one you are. How do you think I must feel?"

24

Mangala decided to concentrate on her driving and not get into any argument with her sister.

After getting stuck in several traffic jams and praying hard that they wouldn't be stopped at any more security checkpoints, they finally reached Saranawila. They drove straight to Maud's house. Mangala rushed to the door and was surprised to find it locked. She walked around the garden looking for Gunapala but there were no signs of him anywhere. Meanwhile Mihiri and Old Maud were waiting in the back seat of the car.

"What's happening Akka ? " shouted Mihiri impatiently, tired of holding Old Maud.

"The door is locked and Gunapala cannot be found" complained a harassed Mangala.

"Why don't you ask the baas who is working on Amila's roof whether he saw Gunapala?" Mihiri said.

Mangala ran up to Amila's house. The baas was adjusting the tiles on the roof.

"Aney baas, did you see Gunapala anywhere?" she tried to sound calm.

The baas looked down and said "Ah yes - Gunapala told me he was going to the kade to get some bulath - he locked the house and took the key with him."

By now, Mihiri looked like she'd been hit by a thunderbolt. She got out of the car. Old Maud was lying down on the seat. Sideways. Her legs dangling.

"Where are you going - instead of helping me?" Mihiri snapped.

"Where- where are we going to put the body?" asked Mangala.

"We'll just put her - er - it - on a chair -on the verandah - otherwise where? That fool Gunapala won't come back for hours if I know him."

They laboured with Old Maud. Although she was a frail old lady while alive, her dead body was an unbelievable weight, and it took all their strength to manoeuvre her out of the car. The corpse leaned heavily against Mihiri while Mangala ran in and brought one of the chairs. They sat her on the chair and heaved the great load onto the little verandah.

The tinkle of a bell made them jump. It was only the postman.

"Only one letter for the Loku Nona today!" he said chirpily to Old Maud. "Loku Nona won't talk to me today" continued the postman. "She is not looking so well no?" he remarked. "Aiyo she is fast asleep also!"

"Yes yes- she can't talk to you today" said Mangala hastily collecting the letters before he came up the steps to give them to her.

Amila's baas came up to them. "Ah the Loku Nona is back - is she alright now?" he asked. He was too close to them for the sisters to avoid telling him the truth.

" She is back - but she is dead" mumbled Mangala.

"If she is dead why is she sitting on the chair?" queried the baas in a tone of total disbelief. "Dead people can't sit!" he scoffed.

"We wanted to put her on her bed but the door is locked so we have to put her on the chair." Mangala explained as calmly as she could.

"Why don't you go and look for Gunapala?" suggested Mihiri.

The baas took off. He meandered down the road stopping every now and then to talk to whoever passed him.   Mangala and Mihiri watched him intently. They had no choice but to sit on the verandah with Maud. Old Maud's eyes were closed and she looked like she had just fallen asleep on the chair. The baas returned in about half an hour. He could not find Gunapala anywhere. Mangala and Mihiri were at their wits end. Mangala had developed a severe migraine and decided to go home and rest.

"I'd better go and call the nieces." said Mihiri and went with Mangala back to their house.

Old Maud was left on her own, sitting on a chair, well propped up with cushions. Mihiri tried calling the Nieces but there was no response. She decided to drive down to their place and meet them.

Amila was returning home from school, taking refuge from the scorching sun under the shade of her umbrella. She spotted Maud seated on her verandah and waved to her. Maud did not wave back. She must be sleeping, or maybe she didn't see me, thought Amila. She got back home, and went outside to see what the baas was doing.

"Fine thing happened today no lady," he said, "that old lady next door fell down." He mumbled while filling his mouth with his chew of betel.

"She must be alright because I saw her just now." said Amila.

"Ah no," said the baas his mouth full. " She is dead."

Amila looked up in surprise. "Dead?" she questioned. "But I just saw her seated on the verandah and waved to her. Dead people don't sit up on chairs!" she exclaimed.

"That's the thing. That's what I also said. Anyway," he sloshed his mouth up and down, "anyway, she is sitting on a chair on the verandah but she is dead. Aiyo I don't know where Gunapala is - those two missis can't put the old lady on the bed because he has locked the door and gone somewhere." the baas explained his mouth still busy.

Amila rushed across to Mangala's house. She banged on the door and woke up Mangala. "Mangala you can't leave old Maud on the verandah" she remonstrated, "- I mean if she's dead - er - is she dead?"

"Yes, such a mess!" replied Mangala, holding her throbbing head. "Couldn't contact the nieces also, so Mihiri has gone to see whether she could bring them over."

"Missi was looking for me?" It was Gunapala. He was surprised that he had been missed.

The baas came running up "Gunapala Aiya, the old lady is dead no!"

"Dead?" said Gunapala in surprise. "But - I just saw her sitting outside when I was coming - only thing she was sleeping so I didn't disturb her."

Amila and Mangala went to Old Maud's place. They had to get her onto her bed, before her nieces arrived! Gunapala opened the door and all of them carried the old lady on the chair into her bedroom. They heaved the body onto her bed. Her hands fell heavily on the sides, just hanging down like two leaden poles. Amila managed to fold Old Maud's arms across her chest. Mangala went back home to rest. Gunapala stood leaning against the door. Amila sat with Old Maud.

There was a crunch on the gravel and the two nieces walked in. They sobbed and ran to their aunt and held her.

"I met one of the neighbours at the entrance," said Niece Number One. "They said they saw her sitting on the verandah just a while ago."

"We never knew she had a heart problem - this must have been her first attack." echoed Niece Number Two.

Amila remained silent. She realised that it was time for her to leave.

Camping Calamities

Charming Charismus loved the jungle. He loved the trees and plants, and the little leeches that clung to his legs and the friendly frogs that leapt on him from nowhere. The humming of the mosquitoes, who were busily distributing malignant malaria or deadly dengue to the visitors sounded like music to his ears. And therefore, what he enjoyed most in life was to gather his friends together and take off on a camping trip. The wilds made him go wild with joy, and whenever the opportunity came his way, he dashed off to enjoy nature in its natural state. They would take their food and tents and beds and every imaginable thing they would need for their week-end sojourn in the jungle. As he was a person of great method and discipline, he organised his party to the last box of matches, and there was never a hitch in the arrangements. They always had a wonderful time. Not only did they enjoy their surroundings, but had the luxury of dining al fresco and indulging in delicacies like Chocolate Mousse with cream topping and drinking Gin Slings and Bloody Marys right there in the middle of the jungle. It was indeed an idyllic situation.

Last weekend he and his Beloved Inura got together with a crowd of friends and took off to the Wild Life Sanctuary. This special place not only boasted of elephants and deer and bear and peafowl, but also more recently recorded the presence of strange striped two legged feline beasts who prowled these very same jungles, and scared to death the visitors who dared to enter its tangled and densely wooded portals.

The first day went by with no hint of excitement and the group had relaxed to the point where they were talking to the trees and telling the peafowl how beautiful they were. While Charming Charismus as Chief Organiser, was seeing to the food and other necessities, his Beautiful Beloved Inura relaxed in a hammock, dozing off from time to time and doing little else. The friends in the group were relaxing with drinks in their hands and recalling all sorts of incredible stories which they had encountered during previous camping trips. The children were happily playing childhood games, which the adults had now forgotten, as childhood was something way back in their past, too long ago to be remembered. Upon this happy scene of comradely conversation, the tinkling of children's laughter, and the regular hum of the Beautiful Beloved Inura breathing peacefully in her hammock, a sudden piercing scream rent the air, shattering the peace and harmony that prevailed. Everybody stopped what they were doing -except of course the Beautiful Inura.

Charismus, who was in charge, rushed to the spot from whence came the scream, and was shocked to find the cook in a state of collapse. He just managed to pick him up and place him on a nearby chair when a low grunt made him look up. His state of shock intensified when there before him, stood a big black bear eyeing him with a threatening look. Meanwhile, the others had assembled their mobility and rushed to the scene, only to be rooted again by what they beheld. By now the women and children who had also ventured to see the cause for the scream, yelled till their lungs nearly burst, when they saw the Black Hulk. It was a big, black, burly bear - with not the slightest resemblance to the lovable Winnie the Pooh. He took a step forward and opened his mouth in a deep growl, showing a set of formidable fangs which filled his ample mouth. He put up a paw, gesticulating that either he was calling them or telling them to get lost. The claws at the end of his paw were several inches long and nicely curved, specially designed of course, for tearing things apart. With all the mayhem taking place around him, Charismus who was in charge remember, and who was not only charming but coolheaded as well, had to take things in his control or all would have been lost to this Dark Monster. His mind raced forwards and backwards and his brain was calling upon all its resources for some immediate action. Aha! He suddenly remembered the crackers. He always carried crackers with him, not just the eating kind but the good cheena pattas rachinna kind - just in case they had to celebrate some important occasion or another.

He lit some of these and flung them towards the bear, who was puzzled at first and then realizing that these things sparked and ran about, immediately scuttled away from them and took refuge in the forest. He turned and looked at them a couple of times, but a few more of the cheena pattas were thrown in his direction, and he decided to play safe and get well away from these mad humans who not only shrieked hysterically but were also rude enough to throw things at him which made such an unpleasant din. No need to get mixed up with that lot! Once the bear left, Charismus had to tend to the ladies who had fainted in fright and the children who had to be comforted. He was greatly relieved to find that his Beautiful Beloved Inura had just awoken from her slumber, saying she had had a bad dream which was full of cheena pattas noises, so much so, it woke her up.

Meanwhile, in another part of the forest, some cute kellas and kapati kollas were having a river bath. The kellas were clad in colourful diya reddas and looked quite becoming as they frolicked in the water, chatting with one another and laughing merrily. Suddenly their revelry was interrupted by a kind of patta-patta noise, which sounded like gunhots. To them the only shots from the jungle would be from the Two Legged Striped Cats who were haunting the area and ready to shoot at the drop of a leaf. They were petrified when they heard more reports, and jumped helter skelter out of the river and ran as fast as their feet could carry them, shrieking and crying out loudly for their lives to be saved.

While Charismus was tending to the faint and weak hearted in his camp he suddenly spotted, through the shrub of the forest a band of fleeing human beings, crying out for mercy and what have you. Oh - they must have been scared by the crackers, thought Charismus. They must have thought they were gunshots, said someone. They must have thought they were being attacked by the Striped Cats! Charismus, who was in charge remember, had to come into action again. He leapt into his Intercooler Jet Propelled Four Wheeled Winged Charger with his friend Hairy (named after the hirsute chest he displayed), and dashed off to catch up with the terrified group, in order to assuage their fears.

The frightened and fleeing bathers now sensed that there was some Monstrous Thing rushing behind them, and the driver was waving frantically to them. Their fears were intensified when they saw that seated next to the driver was a big black hairy- chested man who was also waving his arms up and down. They were certain that these were the Striped Cats chasing them in one of their contraptions. They feared they would be captured and killed - or worse captured and tortured. They ran even faster and cried out even louder and the whole forest rang out with their pleas for mercy.

Meanwhile, the Warden was having his afternoon siesta. He had spent all morning filling in documents giving details of Visitors to the Sanctuary, and was mentally and physically exhausted. Besides, it was a hot day and he had decided to take forty winks or maybe just a little more, on his litttle buru ande which was on the other side of his desk. He was snoring deeply and was rudely awakened when Tracker Hendirick burst into his office, eyes bulging and gasping like he was about to take his last breath.

"Whass - whass the problem?" the Warden asked sitting up and rubbing his eyes which were still full of sleep.

"Aiyo Sir, I don't know, it seems some tigers are chasing some people who were bathing in the wewa near the Camping grounds."

"What tigers man? We are having only leopards no – from where tigers?"

"Not animal tigers Sir, those other –" he held out a trembling hand and rolled his eyes to indicate what he meant.

The Warden sat up in a trice, fully awake, when he realized what Hendirick was talking about. "Where – where are they?"

"Just near the wewa Sir. They are in one of those big Intercooler things chasing the people who were bathing. Those are running without any clothes also, and screaming like mad. The people who are chasing are a dangerous bunch no Sir – now what to do?"

The Warden was exasperated – why the heck did they have to come to his area and create this rumpus. He had to do something. He climbed into his Jeep and with Hendirick next to him, drove to the Camping Area to see what the hullabaloo was about. On his way there he encountered the Terrified Bathers and Charming Charismus and his Hairy Chested Friend in their runabout and chase-around activities and he promptly halted both parties. Charming Charismus waved gaily to him.

"Ah – Warden – good we met you – these people are thinking we are chasing them but we are trying to stop them from running."

"We are running because you are chasing us no – you are driving fast behind us – so you are chasing no." A burly male had come forward from the Bathers.

The Warden listened to this exchange of words and could not help but observe, that most of them, as Hendirick had aptly described, were as bare as on the day on which they were born. He found it difficult to take his eyes away from the scene before him and snarled at Charismus who was tapping him on his shoulder.

" So -what are you doing- chasing these people?" he demanded. Whereupon, the whole story was repeated for the Warden. He then told the Bathers to return to their Bungalows or wherever they had come from, and assured them that the shot were not gun shots but crackers sent off by Charming Charismus himself. At this revelation, they promptly collapsed in relief and had to be piled into the Warden's Jeep to be transported to their destination.

Charming Charismus smiled his usual disarming smile and tried to explain further to the Warden, but such as Fate would have it, the Warden, now weighed down with the Fleeing Bathers and seized by an uncontrollable burst of temper, was in no mood to pay heed to Charismus. Instead, he grabbed the poor Charmer and threw him also into the Jeep, first handcuffing him securely lest he should escape and cause further problems in the Forest.

Word of this incident got around to the Concerned Campers, and they rushed to rescue their Leader and Friend from the vicious clutches of the Warden. Charming Charismus could never understand what betook the Warden to behave in such an unfair and strange manner, after all, he did try to do something good and worthwhile. He shook his head in disbelief at the irrationality of human behaviour and went to search for his Beloved Inura, who was of course enjoying a deep slumber in her hammock and smiling sweetly at her pleasant dreams.

Fair Exchange

There was great consternation in the Millawanna household. Lorinda had run away with her boyfriend in the early hours of the morning. A note on her pillow read, "Darling Amma and Appachchi, I am going to marry my true love Benildus. Your loving daughter, Lorinda."

Lorinda was the elder daughter of Milton and Dulcie. Milton was a prosperous businessman in the little town of Bolawatte. He sold dud cars to customers and then repaired them, making a very lucrative turnover.

Milton had discovered the name Lorinda in a magazine, advertising the latest soft drink in some place in South America. As the years went by Lorinda became taller and wider and showed signs of reaching Amazonian proportions. Eight years later their second daughter Aloris was born. The unusual name derived from the fact that when Dulcie's cousins, who were visiting from Los Angeles saw this dark brown baby with enormous eyes, one of them remarked, "My child she is just like a loris!" Dulcie immediately presumed that Aloris must be some famous film star from Hollywood, and thus named her little angel so.

It was Jacintha, the longstanding maid of the Millawanna household, who had discovered that Lorinda was missing. She had taken Lorinda her "bed tea" and was shocked to find the room empty of its occupant. Dulcie was in a deep sleep, her loud snores reverberating across the room, when Jacintha burst into her room shrieking out her discovery. Dulcie woke up with a start to find a hysterical Jacintha thrusting a note into her hands, which made her burst into a flood of tears.

"Aiyoo, what am I to do, such a shame for us," she wailed, her plump body convulsing with anguish.

Milton was in a shocked state. The twitch in his eye became aggravated at the news, and he looked like he was constantly winking. What a terrible shame for them. How was he going to sort out the wedding which they had planned - only a month away? What was he going to tell the bridegroom, Placidus Pelawatte who was his friend Justin's son? Justin was, after all, a man of importance - a Member of Parliament to be exact. Milton swore under his breath at his elder daughter for putting him into this embarrassing position. To add to everything he couldn't think straight what with Dulcie screaming and crying all the time.

He went into his office room and sat down at his desk and held his bald head, which shone like a polished coconut shell. He massaged it gently. Massaging his head always seemed to bring about all sorts of new ideas, and true to form, an idea slowly emerged. Why not, he thought. Yes, why not give his younger daughter in marriage instead of the older one? After all, they were from the same family, and Aloris could be considered marriageable as she had just passed her 'O' Levels. Also the groom would get the same dowry- house, coconut property and a car. He patted the handlebar moustache which decked his upper lip, and rushed off to speak to Dulcie.

"Dulcie, will you stop this crying. I have something to tell you." Dulcie promptly contained her sobs and listened.

"About the wedding Dulcie,..." he started.

"Aiyoo - don't mention the wedding, such a shame for us- duwa running away like this." She broke into sobs again.

"Dulcie listen, will you!" Milton ordered.

Dulcie sniffled.

"I have the solution," Milton announced. "No need to get excited and tell everyone about this Lorinda's nonsense. We can give Aloris to marry Placidus no? After all, he won't lose anything on the deal, so what's the difference? Aloris is also our daughter, and someday we will have to find a husband for her no? So now we have found one. I will speak to Justin, I'm sure it will be all right." So saying, he marched out of the room and called Jinadasa to bring the Benz.

Meanwhile, the commotion had woken up Aloris, who had rushed out of her room to find her mother and Jacintha seated on the back verandah in hysterical duet.

"Aney - what's happened?" she asked.

When they informed her, she stayed calm. Thank goodness she's gone, she thought. Only that fool Benildus will run away with my sister! Aloris smiled inwardly. How they tried to marry Lorinda to Placidus. Her Placi. When she first saw him she knew she had to have him. His tall muscular figure and curly long hair made her head spin. In turn, Placidus couldn't take his eyes off Aloris. Her flashing dark eyes, long tresses and well moulded figure made his knees quake. He had been proposed to Lorinda even though he cringed at the very sight of her. But what to do? At least the dowry was good.

Aloris rushed into the bathroom, locked the door and turned on the shower. She whisked the mobile 'phone out of her dressing gown pocket and dialled Placi's number. The ring of the telephone by his bed woke him up. He was so thrilled to hear the voice of his beloved Aloris.

"Hello my little sweetie, you woke me up, but so nice to hear your tinkling voice no!"

"Here Placi, don't talk nonsense aney," said Aloris, "you don't know what has happened - Akka has run off with that Benildus!"

"What?" Placidus sat up in bed. "My gosh, then how to have the wedding?"

The line was cut because the battery was dead.

A few hours later Milton reappeared with a satisfied look on his face.

Dulcie was resting on her bed, her eyes red and swollen.

"Ah, Dulcie, not to worry. I have fixed everything. I spoke to Justin and he said it was no problem if Aloris was proposed to his son, as long as the dowry remains the same. He said he'll tackle the boy. We have to tackle the girl, so Dulcie now get up will you."

They sent for Aloris. She seemed melancholy and downcast, and raised her eyes sadly to look at her parents.

"Aney Appachchi, I heard all about this Akka's running away. I don't know how she could've done this to us. Now what will happen to the wedding." As she spoke her heart beat hard against her breast.

"Duwa we have thought about it and Amma and I thought best thing if you can get married to Placidus - after all he's a good catch and his father is a very important person also. So that's the best thing to do." Milton and Dulcie glanced at each other, praying that Aloris would agree with their plan.

"Appachchi and Amma I'll do anything you tell me. You know I'll always listen to you." She looked down and wiped an imaginary tear from her eye.

Dulcie let out a sob of relief "Duwa I will give you anything you want."

"In that case Amma, I'd like to have the emerald set," Aloris replied quickly. The emerald set once belonged to Dulcie's grandmother and was a prized family heirloom. Dulcie hesitated- but only for a moment- for the family reputation had to be saved at any cost. Milton rubbed his head, relieved that the wedding could take place as planned.

That evening Placidus came over to meet his new bride. Their coy glances belied their secret desires, as they sat together on the big settee in the hall. Their parents sat with them and they discussed the plans for the wedding.

Next day Lorinda returned with Benildus clutching her arm. Milton and Dulcie, though angry at what she had done, were much relieved to see her. Dulcie immediately broke out into a state of weeping and Milton with his eye twitching non stop gave them a strong lecture on how children should conduct themselves, daughters in particular. Aloris smirked at the way Benildus hung on every word her sister said and at the way her sister gazed at him in return. Jacintha peering from the doorway, just wrung her hands up and down stopping only to wipe the tears which were beginning to trickle down her face. The runaway couple repented their thoughtless behaviour and begged forgiveness. Matters were sorted out amicably and they all agreed that the most important thing was the fact that the family name had been saved. Soon the Millawanna household was immersed in the preparations for their younger daughter's marriage.

The wedding was a lavish affair. The whole town of Bolawatte and many important businessmen and politicians from the capital were also present. The guests had plenty to eat and drink and the band played Milton's favourite bailas which prompted him to sing along as he danced. Dulcie's happiness made her shed many tears again, and her red swollen eyes gave her a strange oriental appearance. Lorinda sat close to Benildus in a secluded corner. People remarked that not only did Aloris and Placidus make a handsome couple, but that already they looked so much in love with each other.

The Chimes of Time

Milton was quite concerned. He had heard a radio announcement saying that the time was being put forward by one hour. So now, if it was five o'clock they were going to make it six o'clock. But to his mind, five o'clock was five o'clock, so how could it be six? He could not figure it out at all. First the power cuts and now this. Life was becoming very complicated indeed. He sighed and reached for his briefcase. Maybe he should go home immediately and give the bad news to his wife, Dulcie. He had better break it gently, as Dulcie would, he was certain, burst into tears the way she did at everything. He had not changed the time on his watch. He looked at it and it said five thirty. So if it was really six thirty he was very late to get home. Or was it five thirty - even he was not sure. Better go, he thought, otherwise Dulcie would be furious - she hated him coming late.

When he got home there was pandemonium. As he stepped into the house, he heard Dulcie wailing.

"What, what has happened?" he asked Jacintha the maid.

"Aney , I don't know - something about them taking all our clocks to do something or another."

He rushed into the bedroom to find Dulcie in a terrible state.

"Aiyo Milton, now they are saying that the time has changed - they are saying we are going to get some more daylight - I can't with this. First it is dark with the power cuts now they are trying to catch the daylight. So dangerous no! To dabble in these things. Don't know what might happen." she sniffled into a handkerchief.

"Now now Dulcie - nothing to get excited about. They are just putting the time forward by one hour - that's all. Just remember that when it is four it is five and when it is five it is really four. Quite simple." Milton explained in a tone of feigned confidence.

"So then is it really five or four - aney I'll never know." she whimpered.

Gunadasa knocked at the door.

"What is it?" asked Milton.

"The next-door gentleman wants to know whether you can give him a clock, because their ones are all at the old time, and he wants to put the new time on, so he thought better to do it with a different clock, so that the times don't get mixed up." Gunadasa explained.

Milton practically threw the bedside clock at him. "Give this to them. Why can't they buy a new clock instead of taking my clock, I don't know!" he ranted.

Cuthbert and Mildred Jethuwana from next door visited them that evening. Cuthbert was a short stout man and fair complexioned. He tried very hard to cover his receding hairline by combing the few strands of hair he possessed, horizontally, across his head. Mildred resembled her husband in stature and colour. Her striking feature was her bulging eyes, which enabled her to snoop on all the neighbourhood activities.

"Aney, thank you for the clock!" exclaimed Mildred. "Now we have both times in the house - just in case we suddenly want to find out the real time, we have to look at our old clock over the dining table. Your clock with the new time we put in the kitchen. So easy for us now! Only thing is, we have a real problem you know. Now when Bubby Girl gets married next month we won't know when the real nakath time is - the old time or the new time. We might have to do everything twice I think. I don't know what we're going to do!" She sounded really troubled about this.

Cuthbert Jethuwana prided himself on being well read and well informed. "I was reading somewhere the other day, that when in Sri Lanka it is five o'clock evening time, in Australia they are ten o'clock night time, and in England they are twelve o'clock lunchtime - on the same day. How can that be? We all have to be the same time no - after all this is one world no? I wrote a stinker to their Letters to the Editor page - must see what happens."

Milton and Dulcie were quite impressed. "You actually wrote to the Editor?" asked Dulcie seriously, implying that next to God, the Editor was the most powerful entity.

"Told him what I thought of the whole situation." went on Cuthbert, with pride in his voice.

"Another thing, last time we went to the Holy Land, all the way on the plane the Captain or some chap was telling us that the time was being changed. Cuthbert and I of course didn't take any notice. We kept our watches to the real time. I mean if in Sri Lanka we can have the correct time why should we bow down to some foreigner who tells us some time or the other?" recalled Mildred.

"These foreigners, they are always trying to tell us what to do. They don't realise we had kings and advanced irrigation systems before their countries even came into existence. Now they are trying to tell us about this time and that time. I of course won't fall for those tricks!" said Cuthbert, a note of defiance in his voice. "I was also thinking, all this extra time they are giving - maybe at the end of the year we will have one extra month also. In twelve years I will be one year younger!" he beamed with his statements of mathematical insight.

There was a pause while the others digested these words of wisdom.

"That is of course quite true" they agreed in unison, fanning themselves against the stifling heat and trying to keep away the mosquitoes, who were droning around them in hordes and having their little bloody drinks at every turn.

Jacintha had made hoppers for dinner.

"Why are we eating so early?" asked Milton, "my watch says seven o'clock."

"But that time near the table is eight no - can't you remember, you changed it this evening?" replied Dulcie.

"Ah yes - anyway - better wait till eight thirty then - because then it is really seven thirty no. How to eat so early as seven!" Milton laughed nervously.

Suddenly the lights went off. Jacintha ran into the dining room, almost knocking over a chair - "I don't know what happened I was just taking an appa off the cooker when - takkas - the lights went off! Also I was in the middle of making the papaw drink in the liquidiser." Her voice came out from the darkness like some ghostly spirit.

"This is the electricity cut." explained Milton.

"But that is at eight o'clock no - now it is only seven." she intoned.

"But the new time is eight no - so how can it be seven?" Milton snapped irritated.

"Anyway they can't just cut the lights like this and like that - now see no papaw drink also. Aney, don't know what has happened to the TV shows now that the times are different. Such a nuisance!" grumbled Jacintha.

Milton and Dulcie went to bed at nine thirty - their usual bed time.

"How to sleep so early aiyo - its really eight thirty no!" complained Dulcie.

"I am sick of this time business. I am going to sleep whether its eight thirty or nine thirty or whatever. I have to get up early tomorrow because I have a meeting in office at seven."

"Aney sin for you - to have meetings at six in the morning. How hard you have to work Milton." Dulcie's voice had an unmistakable tone of admiration in it.

To Go or Not to Go?

The shrill ring of the telephone jolted Milton. He was having one of his usual "bad dreams", as he described them, where someone was trying to kill him. That was when the 'phone rang. Just as the killer was with his knife poised at Milton's throat.

"Aiyooo—" he screamed, waking not only himself but also Dulcie who was sleeping beside him.

By the time he got his glasses from his bedside table and put them on, the phone had rung about ten times. He looked at the clock. 6.30. Who on earth could be calling him at this ungodly hour - especially on a Saturday - the only day when he could sleep late? Damn it! He couldn't find his hearing aid - where on earth could it be? The 'phone rang on relentlessly. He picked it up but could hardly hear the speaker.

"Hullo hullo - who is it?"

"Milton - this is Bertie - just to tell you men that there is a cordon and search operation on. Don't leave your house - anytime now the authorities will come and ask for your ID card and may want to search your place —"

Milton struggled to catch the phrases."What did you say - Gordon has had his house searched?" Gordon was his neighbour - poor chap to be put into such an embarrassing position.

"Not Gordon, cordon- cordon and search - —"

Dulcie was also wide awake now. "Aney what has happened to poor Gordon?" she queried.

"Shh - " said Milton as now with her prattling, he couldn't hear Bertie at all.

"——get your ID ready and don't leave the house - they will arrest you otherwise—don't leave the house whatever happens ———" Bertie seemed to go on and on.

Milton put the 'phone down.

"What what?" asked Dulcie tugging at his arm.

"It seems Gordon didn't have his ID and has been arrested. But Bertie told us not to leave the house - so what can we do now?"

"Shall we ring Gordon's place and ask that old man who works there what has happened?"

Dulcie dialled Gordon's number. Gordon wasn't there. But Gordon's voice was. The answering machine responded '.......leave your name and number after the long beep.' it said.

Dulcie slammed the phone "Aney I don't know - that old fool is not even answering - that machine of Gordon's is on and I of course can't talk to a machine - so silly no. Don't know what has happened to poor Gordon. Do you think we should go there and find out?"

"But Bertie said not to leave the house. What if the police come here and find us walking around the neighbourhood - they will arrest us also."

"Ah then we might be able to see Gordon - sin no - he's on his own now remember after that wife of his ran off with the driver - he's all alone no."

Milton was in a quandary. Gordon lived right down his road. Should he or should he not take the risk of walking all that way to check on him? The question burned into the nether regions of his mind. He kept rubbing his bald pate as though, like the magic lamp, it would produce a genie who could help him.

"Shall we send Jacintha to find out?" asked Dulcie.

"What difference does that make? Jacintha can also get arrested if she is caught outside the house. No no - we better stay in."

"But poor Gordon no - after all he is our neighbour also. I know what! Shall I ring the Police Station and ask them?"

"No no let me do that." said Milton hastily, fearing what further trouble they would get into if he let Dulcie call the Police.

Complaining to Dulcie that he couldn't find his hearing aid anywhere, he called the Police Station.

"Hullo hullo - is that the Inspector?"

"Inspector - inspector of what?"

"Ah yes Inspector - just to find out whether there is one Gordon there? He was arrested this morning?"

"You want Inspector Gordon? I say - isn't that Milton? Milton this is not the Police Station - this is Piya speaking - what has happened to Gordon?"

Piya was his friend who lived nearby.

"Piya - my God! Did they arrest you also? Didn't you hear that Gordon was also arrested? Were you together?

"Milton - I'm not at the police station? What's all this about being arrested?"

"Hullo hullo -Piya - stay on there - I will speak to the inspector myself and try and get all of you out." He slammed down the phone.

"It seems Piya is also at the police station and all of them have been arrested. We have to go and rescue them. Come Dulcie - we cannot think of whether it is safe for us to go or not to go. The fact is, our good friends are in trouble and need our help. We have to take the risk."

The decision made, both Milton and Dulcie made haste to rescue their friends.

Dulcie was putting on her final touch of lipstick with Milton impatiently pacing up and down waiting for her.

"Dulcie what is this - you're not going to a party to dress up like that!" Milton exclaimed when he saw Dulcie in a frothy pink saree which made her look like a walking marshmallow.

"Must look good for the Police no - otherwise they will think we are also riff-raff and might even arrest us! Milton, here take your hearing aid – I found it under the bed - otherwise you won't know what the inspector is saying."

Jacintha was hovering outside the gate, looking out for the police who were supposed to raid their house anytime now. She had her ID in her hand all set and ready so that there wouldn't be any problems when they arrived.

Milton and Dulcie stopped the car near the gate.

"Jacintha - go inside otherwise you'll be caught by the police for being outside no!"

Jacintha scuttled into the safety of the house.

"Aiyo sin no for Gordon mathaththaya!" she exclaimed to Gunadasa who was having his cup of tea on the back verandah.

Gunadasa just nodded.

"Don't know what he was doing on the road no - so early in the morning.

"What a terrible thing to happen to Gordon! Poor chap! Which police station is he at?" he asked hastily, a worried look on his face.

"He's at Bolgoda," replied Milton.

"I didn't know there was a police station at Bolgoda - so so -what's the latest on him?"

"No no - not at the police station - he's at his estate at Bolgoda. Piya - how did you manage to get out of the police station?"

"What police station?" Piya asked puzzled.

"Where you were locked up," said Dulcie.

"I wasn't locked up!" exclaimed Piya in amazement.

Milton and Dulcie looked at each other quite perplexed.

"I thought you rang up from the Police Station," said Milton.

"Police Station? Nonsense! You were the one asking for the Police station - why you told me about Gordon also! I thought Gordon had got caught up in this cordon and search operation they had this morning," explained Piya.

"Cordon and search?" Milton and Dulcie said in unison.

"Yes yes - there was a search this morning - they blocked roads and also visited houses in many areas - searching for terrorist suspects."

Dulcie looked disapprovingly at Milton. Milton looked sheepish. He rubbed his head. "Ah I must have heard cordon as Gordon - so what can I do. I must have heard wrong - without my hearing aid, what to do?" he mumbled, as they walked into the house.

The Writer

The verandah was cool - the big trees protected it from the searing sun. Alex was relaxing on his lounge, with a beer by his side and the latest bestseller in his hands. *I wish I could write like Jeffry Doyle!* He always wanted to be a writer - he had tried his hand at short stories but hadn't published anything- as yet. What he had written so far seemed stale stuff. He was looking for something different.

Loud voices disturbed him. He grunted with irritation and put the book down. These new neighbours were a pest - always arguing - more like fighting really. They went on endlessly almost all day long - and often right into the night. He got up and went into his study. Standing by the window he was surprised when he discovered he could see right into their downstair sitting room. The man and the woman were yelling at each other. Then the idea came in a flash - like one of those blinding bursts of lightning. *Why, here was the perfect source of material for his book!*

He listened with careful attention to every word they spoke. He watched every movement that was within his line of vision. Soon he became a veteran eavesdropper. He found that all the time they spent fighting, he spent peeping and listening by his window. He would wake up each morning and watch the clock, walk to the window and peer out, jump out of his chair at the slightest sound from next door. *I must meet them - then I could have a better perspective of the whole situation. Yes, I'll just walk across and have a chat. It would help give my characters more depth if I actually knew them.*

He could hardly stand still as he rang the doorbell. A woman opened the door. She was small and delicate boned and had short dark hair. Her eyes had a slant to them - oriental, definitely. When she smiled he saw white even teeth. Her full lips moved up and down. He realised that he hadn't heard a word she'd said when he found her staring at him with a quizzical look on her face. He held out his hand, "I'm Alex Fernandesz from next door - thought I'll just come over and say 'Hi'."

"I'm Celine Watson." Her voice was low and soft -' seductive' he decided, would be the right word.

Celine Watson, he mentally rolled the name on his tongue. Then the man came forward. Was this her husband - or a lover? So many possibilities,

"Who the hell is this?" The husband's voice.

"Why - why it's just a friend - you know- my - friend's - er Jeannie's brother." she said in a voice that faltered.

"A friend - with his arms round you? What kind of a friend is that?" the husband bellowed.

"Calm down - I've got to go anyhow - it was not what you think it is —" the young man tried to get a word in.

The burly husband had had too much of this. He struck out with all his might and knocked the young man over - flat on the floor.

The girl screamed. "Oh - oh - "she knelt down beside the fallen man, then "he's not breathing."

"Serves him damn well right!"

The girl stood up, looking distraught -"He's - he's -dead - I think - you did it - you horrid .... you brute ...you've killed him!"

"Oh shut up!"

The adrenalin was flowing fast. Alex knew he had to get away quickly. His fingers trembled as he crept out of the gate. He went past his house right up to the junction where the shops were. People were still on the streets standing around in groups, talking to one another; some were hurrying by with bags full of shopping strung on their arms. The fluorescent lights of the wayside eating houses cast a garish hue on the surroundings. He walked fast but tried to keep a steady pace. He could feel his heart hammering against his chest. It was past midnight when he got back home. He went straight to his darkened study and looked out. The house next door was in complete darkness. Not a sound emanated from it. It was as though it was as dead as the inert body that must have been lying on the sitting room floor. What would they do with the body? Get rid of it of course, but how? Bury it - put it into the boot of the car and drive off to hide it someplace, he wondered? What about blood? He felt sick at the idea of blood splattered all over. He shuddered at the million possibilities that flooded his mind, as he sat at the computer. He had to get on with his story. His fingers raced feverishly over the keys and at almost three in the morning he punched out the last line - the grand finale - the climax. Then he poured himself his fifth cup of coffee, leaned back in his chair, and fell fast asleep.

Next day when he awoke it was past midday. The sun was shining brazenly into the room. Hurrying to the window, he peered out. Not a thing- all shut. I'll just have to go across. He must have rung the bell a good half dozen times - but the place was absolutely silent. They must have got away, but what about the body? He held his breath as he stole over to their garden and walked round the house. Not a sound. He peered through the slats of the garage door – no car. I was right, they've just taken off. My God, they've really scooted. But what's happened to Celine - what if that brute of a husband knocked her out too? His stomach churned at the thought. Maybe I should call the police?

He went back to his computer. 'Police' he typed with a question mark at the end of it. He stared at the screen, drumming his fingers on the table - his brain now a frenzy of images.

'He called the police from a call box round the corner.' he typed. Sounded good. Yes that's it, he thought. He dashed out and reached the call box at the junction. His hands were sweating so much he had to wipe them with his handkerchief. Then he remembered the old trick - and placed his handkerchief over the mouthpiece when he made his call.

He changed his voice and spoke slowly -"Murder at number 16 Medler Street" was his laconic message. He replaced the receiver quickly and turned around to find two ladies staring at him, curious at the handkerchief draped over the 'phone.

Rushing back home he grabbed a glass of beer and settled down on the lounge with the best-seller he was half way through. Now all he had to do was wait, wait for the police to arrive next door.

The minutes seemed like hours, like days almost.

Finally he dozed off on the chair and was startled to find someone waking him up.

Two policemen. What? Then he remembered.

"We had a call reporting a murder here." said one of them.

"Here? A murder? Here?" Alex jumped off the chair.

"Hmm - yes - number 16 isn't it?"

"Yes yes -"

Fall to Happiness

It was an extraordinary way to die. Bizarre, in fact. There he was, just minding his business and walking along happily, when all of a sudden something came crashing down on him. It was one of the workers from the building site immediately above him. The man dropped from the topmost floor, three storeys up, right onto Bandula. They crumpled in a tangled heap onto the road. In a few seconds a crowd gathered, gazing aghast at the two bodies lying there in a bloody mess. Someone put them into a three-wheeler and took them to the hospital.

Bandula was in a bad state when they reached the hospital. Naturally. He was the fallee. The man fallen upon. Moreover, he was a man who looked more like a skeleton. His body was sparsely covered with flesh and skin. When he moved you could almost hear his bones rattle. On the other hand, Indoris, the faller, possessed the proportions of a baby elephant. He weighed as much and looked like one too, what with his enormous pot belly and big round shoulders. So Bandula didn't have a chance. Right from the moment Indoris took that faulty step out of the third floor and plummeted through the air, Bandula, who had taken that fateful step forward directly in alignment with the hunk from space, was a dead man. The noise was terrible. Bandula screamed- a sharp short piercing yell before he was snuffed out. Indoris' cry was longer. It lasted from the third floor right to the time he crashed down on his unfortunate victim. The thud with which he landed created reverberations similar to an earthquake.

Indoris was full of bumps and bruises and a few broken bones, but Bandula was literally crushed to death. At the hospital they couldn't even do a proper post-mortem, as was the custom for patients brought in dead on admission. His bones had been broken into countless fragments and the rest of him was just a messy hotch-potch. Indoris was in a terrible state of shock, for now they did not know whether he had committed murder, manslaughter - or whether it was just a case of accidental death.

In the usual manner, Bandula's wife and family were duly informed about his untimely demise. At three o'clock in the afternoon just as Menike was about to make herself a cup of tea she spotted some policemen at her gate. They showed her Bandula's identity card which they had retrieved from his pocket and told her the bad news. Poor Menike was stunned. She always knew that Bandula was a bit of a fool, but did he have to die like this? Imagine her plight if the neighbours got to know.

Within minutes they were at her doorstep to find out what the police were doing there.

"Aiyo" wailed Menike, "my poor Bandula, met with an - er- accident and died. What am I going to do -with these two children also to look after?" she continued to cry.

She managed to have a quiet word with her friend Kusuma from nextdoor.

"What aney if he was knocked down by a car it would have been much better. What a shame for me to have to live with this - imagine my husband dying because a man fell on top of him? If it was a rock or something like that even it wouldn't have mattered - but a workman? Such a disgrace for us. His brother also fell into a drain and died and his mother tripped over a flower pot and cracked her head and died. Aiyo, what kind of a moosala family I have married into I don't know!" she lamented.

She had to stop the truth from coming out.

Fortunately the coffin was sealed so that the neighbours couldn't ask too many questions. By the time the funeral came around the story was that Bandula was walking down some road when a car came out from nowhere and knocked him dead. By the end of the funeral, it was a broad road and a brand new Mercedes Benz car. A few days later the road was in Colombo 7 and the car was owned by Tilak Mudalali - the richest car Mudalali around. Menike had retrieved her dignity and respect. In fact, it almost seemed like an honour to be killed in such a manner.

Bandula, meanwhile, had taken leave of this unkind world and arrived at the Underworld - not where gangsters and crooks gathered, but more the Homeric Underworld where the dead spent their time wandering around forever and ever and ever. To his great joy he met many of his old friends and family in this unfamiliar place. His brother who had fallen in the drain was also there and greeted him with open arms. So was his mother, the flower-pot tripper. Even she was shocked at what had happened to him.

"Aney putha, you should have found some other way to die no?" she stated.

"So machang, what are you doing now?" Bandula asked his brother.

"Haunting, haunting." he replied.

"Haunting?" Bandula was puzzled.

Anusha smiled at herself in the bathroom mirror, "How lovely to see you- congratulations - how wonderful for you!" she practised in an affected voice. Gihan would be behind her slapping Rohan on the back - really happy for his friend. So I'll go and be nice to every one. What else - might as well enjoy myself.

The Pearl Room at the Sunshine Hotel was crowded when they got there.

"Hullo Derek" Gihan was making his way across the room. Anusha followed. She tripped along, her sari wound tightly round her and allowing her only minute steps.

Derek and Gihan were in serious conversation with each other. Two other men joined them, slapping each other on the shoulder and greeting one another with much joie de vivre. Anusha glued on a smile and tried to attract their attention but they were so engrossed in their conversation they ignored her completely. A group of ladies stood nearby. Go on Anusha go on - join the group. She retrieved her pasty smile and approached the lady in the red silk sari with the big konde.

"Hello - I'm Anusha." Red sari just stared at her as though she had seen a ghost. Anusha looked around the group. Smile smile smile, be friendly - the words ran through her head. They all looked glum and tired. So Anusha switched off the smile and put on a glum and tired look - just so she could be one with them. A waiter floated by with a tray of drinks and she stretched out for a sherry. Now she could drink while looking glum and tired. What a life!

Suddenly across the room she spotted Nalaka. She felt her face blush when she saw him. Her first love- when they were in school. How many years ago? Ten? Twelve? He saw her and waved - she waved back and walked towards him, glancing sideways to see the hawk eyes of the group following her movements.

"Hey Anu - how good to see you!" his arms clasped her and for a moment she thought her hairstyle had come apart, or her sari pota crushed. The old days came tumbling back into her mind and again she felt that queasy sensation in her stomach which made her want to rush to the bathroom. But she had to stay right there, or look a complete ass. So she stayed.

"Yes - good to see you."

He was as handsome as before - filled out but not too fat, just muscular.

We had so much in common - going to the beach, lying in the sun, dancing till dawn, playing tennis almost every evening. He'd given her a gift of a tennis racket for her eighteenth birthday - she'd never forget how he told his father he needed a new racket and got one for her. But he was such a flirt - always had some other girl tagging on even when we were going out.

"So how?" he asked looking her up and down. He put his arm around her. "You're still looking swell. Married?"

"Yes - to Gihan - you remember him?" She tried to wriggle out of his grasp without making too much of a scene.

"Hmm - not really." He pressed her shoulder to him.

Liar - he jolly well must remember Gihan. Hell -this man is a real leech - sorry a lech - lecher.

"Still with the Bank?"

She nodded. "How's everything with you?"

"Couldn't be better. Hey - haven't had a chat for so long - how many years? Ten? Twelve?" He pulled out his card-holder with his free hand, "Gosh I've missed you. Here's my card - call me sometime when you're free. Maybe we could have lunch or go out for a week-end someplace? Recap the old days. You don't have to tell your Gihan." He winked at her.

She cringed. Look at him - hasn't changed much. Even now his eye was wandering around the room, trying to catch an easy prey. My God! Have I fallen into this category? One of his collection? I feel like leaning over and slapping him. Wish I had the guts. But before she could even blink, a shapely sylph dressed in a black and silver chiffon saree with a jacket that was made up of only two thin straps and a band across her chest, sidled up to him. Her smile spread right across her face, lighting up her dark eyes. The shoulder length hair bounced up and down. He let go of Anusha's shoulder and put his arm around the new arrival, holding her waist like he owned her. "Ah Niloo - this is Anu" Anusha winced at the rhyming familiarities he threw at them. He sounded like a collector - this oo and that oo. Horrid. They seem to be engrossed in each other anyway - so I'd better move, Anu thought.

"Must circulate - nice meeting you", she said to them with a laugh. They looked at her and laughed in return. Heart thudding she escaped to the well laid out refreshment tables. Yes I'll have something to eat. She took her time looking over the wide array of eats; there she stood, a solitary figure in the middle of a crowd nibbling chicken wings and sausage rolls and hot hot samosas. She knew no one really cared a jot - but she felt embarrassed standing by herself.

She looked around and decided to venture into another group of ladies. The group of men looked forbidding, what with all their business talk she wouldn't know what to say to them. The ladies were no better. She never knew what to say to them either. She did her usual "Hello I'm Anusha" bit with the smile fixed on her face. They smiled back. Well that's one better than the last lot. She took a bite of the hot hot samosa and could have screamed when her tongue nearly got burnt. Someone was talking to her.

"Do you have any children?" Why did they always ask that? Maybe they knew she was ten years married with no kids. She didn't want them to ask why and probe into all the details of her private life, like they usually did.

"Yes" she replied blithely.

"How many?"

"Two -"

"Girls or boys?"

So damn nosey.

"Girl and boy"

"Ah -how old are they?"

This really was too much. "Mmm -the boy is twelve and the girl is six- they are both in school, they both love swimming and the girl plays tennis for her school - the boy - the boy is-"

"Yes?" large eyes stared at her.

Thoughts flashed through her mind. Shall I say he's a monster with two heads or he's really a girl who pretends to be a boy or he's -"too small to play tennis" she said.

"Ah." Satisfied, her questioner turned to someone else.

Inquisition over; time to go, time to go.

A commotion behind her made her turn around. Nalaka and black chiffon again. A large, rotund, curly haired woman in a long green dress stalked up to him, and with one quick movement slapped him hard and good across his face. He had hardly recovered when she repeated her action on the woman in the black chiffon. It sounded like crackers - patta patta

patta patta. My God this is fun! At least someone has the guts. Anusha stood and stared. The two women were grinding their teeth and calling each other names. They try to keep their voices low but suddenly they lose control and they hit a higher crescendo pitch with every syllable. Two or three gents make an effort to separate them only to be shoved off. Nalaka was nursing his sore cheeks and a bloody nose- too stunned to talk. What a circus, Anusha thought. Nalaka the biggest bloody clown in it. I have to watch this.

"Honey - where were you - I was looking all over–"Look at Gihan searching for her – usually she had to drag him away! What a joke.

"I wanted to tell you I met Nalaka earlier on- he wanted to meet you. What a hullabaloo - he's really in for it." Gihan chuckled.

"What's the row about?"

"Ah - you see he's married to Rohan's sister - she's the one in the green dress"

Oh so that was it. "Who's black chiffon then?"

"Black chiffon?" Gihan was puzzled. "Who's black chiffon? Anyway - we should go - this is disgusting."

"Let's wait - just a bit - this is fun." she grinned and grabbed his hand.

He pulled away. "Oh rubbish - a waste of time -I'll speak to Rohan and wife and meet you outside."

She was so engrossed in what was happening, she started at the tap on her shoulder - Gihan again. "Come on- what's this standing and gaping?" He walked fast, ignoring her, the way he always did when he was annoyed, leaving her scurrying behind.

She opened her bag to take out a tissue and his card fell out floating onto the floor. Placing her stiletto heel on it she ground it hard. There - that's what you deserve, you idiot.

"I thought you hated cocktail parties." was Gihan's snide comment when she reached the car.

"This one was fun Gihan. The food was delicious, the people were interesting in a weird sort of way - and most of all the cabaret was spectacular."

He looked across at her and laughed.

The Wedding

I was rudely awakened from my afternoon siesta by the shrill ring of the telephone.

"We have a wedding to attend today!" Simon's voice sounded extraordinarily calm.

"A wedding? Whose?"

"Golba's son - remember I told you about it some weeks ago? Well, I just found the invitation. It's at 4.30. I'll be there at four." Simon rang off.

My only contact with Golba, who had been in the university with Simon, was when we attended his funeral last year.

It was past 3.30! Now to iron my sari - yards and yards. Dash to the bathroom, stand under the shower turning this way and that to get the soap off, grab the towel and wipe myself in a jiff and then to drape the wretched six yards. Swirl it round and get those little pleats right - and thank God it's okay! Put the hair up in a knot and here's Simon at the door. Flings his briefcase on the bed, runs to the shower splash splash and he's out. Scrambles into clothes, draws fingers through hair and ta da - he's ready.

Jump into the car, rev engine and off we go. The traffic is crawling. Buses, vans, pickups cars all the vehicles in creation are on the road, snarling us up all the way. Weaving this way and that, cursing the heavy blockage on the roads, we finally get to the Church. The car park is full, so we park on the road just outside and dash into the church. As always, Simon storms ahead, while I totter behind in my uncomfortable stiletto heels trying hard not to trip over my sari and make an ass of myself. The Church is packed and we stand stock still just gaping at the crowd, eyes searching for any little gap through which we could creep. Ultimately we settle for two seats at the rear corner. Excusemeexcuseme we mumble as we edge past, treading on toes and sari borders and almost falling over. At last we are there. Two little seats that will hardly hold our bottoms, look at us empty and sad. How the hell do we sit on these? I know, I tell Simon, first I'll sit then you sit, for if both of us sit together we are going to get stuck.

It's almost five o'clock but the bride hasn't turned up as yet. My mind went back to our wedding, when everything was done exactly on time. Was this bride as excited as I was? And the groom - was he chewing his finger nails like Simon did, till his bestman saw his bleeding fingers and shrieked? Oh that was such a long time ago I sighed. I try to shift in my seat but I am well and truly jammed. I'm afraid to stand as the chair might come up with me.

Then suddenly the organ plays the bridal chorus, heralding the arrival of the bride. To stand up is a complicated process and we twist ourselves and managed to get up one at a time. Once on our feet we discover we can't see a thing - not the bride and her entourage, nor the bridegroom who was way up in the front and totally out of sight. All we see is other people. Crushed up against us are saris of silky texture and bright colours and dark jackets and trousers. The smells are a mix of expensive perfumes, cheap scents and strong after shave lotions, making even the simple act of breathing difficult. We have no hymn sheets as they've all been taken. And we are so far back we can hardly hear the proceedings- just a buzz of voices -but thank God the hymns were nice and loud. With nothing to do in between the singing, I decide to look around. I feast my eyes on the beautiful saris. People of all shapes and sizes dressed in their finest, decked in tons of jewellery - earrings, bangles which completely cover their arms and heavy gold chains; perspiration pouring down their faces in the stifling heat. Two little girls in front look behind and giggle. Their mother gives them each a sharp knock, making them burst into tears. I peer to see whether there is anyone I know. Not a single familiar face. Simon is now looking grumpy. He looks down and closes his eyes. Either praying or sleeping. More likely he's sleeping. He does this often. Weddings bore him. He goes for them wishing they were over before he got there. We stand when the others stand and sit when they do- up and down, up and down so many times, each a tight squeeze and making us quite exhausted and sweaty. Simon decides not to stand after three of these and just stays put.

Finally the service ends. I nudge him and he opens his eyes, looking at me as though I had interrupted some sacred contemplation. The organist is bellowing out the bridal march and the couple with their retinue begin walking down the aisle. I crane my neck, and despite my five inch heels can see nothing. Only a sea of heads and multi coloured bodies. I accidentally step on Simon's shoes in the process of trying to stand on my toes. He frowns and mutters.

"Can't you wait till we meet them, instead of standing on my shoes to have a peek?" He peers at his polished shoes which have now been blotched by me.

So I wait and wait. Now we have the impossible task of getting into a line to wish the couple. An avalanche of human beings is upon us, pushing us forward and squashing us hard in between strange people. The strong aroma of sweat and perfume make me feel faint. We inch our way forward, pressed by this great bank of unknown bodies.

Someone nudges me - it's my neighbour Rupa. "I didn't know you knew Cynthy and Kota - they're old friends of ours."

"I thought he was called Golba in school?"

"No -no Kota - because he was so short no."

"Oh?"

She leaned against my ear and whispered "You know that he left her a year ago?"

"Yes – that was so sudden – so sad for them."

Her eyes bulged as she continued to whisper, "But good thing no that just before the wedding he came back – otherwise such a problem for them no?"

"You mean he just – came back- just like that – but-" I slowed down and lost my place in the queue and also lost sight of Rupa.

Then I was heartened by the glimpse of white net - the bride at last! I kiss the smiling bride and wish her everything wonderful. Then the groom. The last time I saw him was at his father's funeral - almost a year ago. He has changed so much. Taller and heavier too - the spurt of adolescence growth, I suppose. A far cry from the skinny little person I had met earlier. He shook my hand and smiled hazily. I turn to move out when I spot Simon - a strange expression on his face. He looks ill. He rushes past me to the car, covering his mouth. I teeter along as fast as I could, heels clipp- clopping along feeling like a Japanese lady in clogs. I am alarmed to find Simon sitting in the car, mumbling incoherently - his face buried in his hands. My God the heat was too much for him. I knew it was far too crowded in there.

"What is it ?" I ask trying to hide my concern.

"It's - its —" he gurgles and splutters.

If it's a heart attack I'm just going to run out and ask for a doctor, there has to be a doctor here somewhere I thought, looking out at the milling throng still winding their way around the church compound.

"What's it dear, are you feeling ill?" my voice assumes a tone of forced calm. "Don't worry - I'll get some help."

"No no! I.." and he collapses into a convulsion of strange utterances.

"What is it?" Now I was really scared, and excited and I wasn't going to hide it. "What's wrong with you?" I demand in a firm strong voice. This nonsense has got to stop.

"Nothing's wrong with me - it's just that, it's just that -its the wrong wedding -we've come to the wrong wedding!" he blurted.

"What? How did that happen?" I retrieved the invitation from the glove compartment.

And so it was. It was the wrong day, and the wrong wedding. Only the church was right!

I sit down next to him. We laugh till we cry, tears pouring down our faces. Passing guests stare curiously into the car.

Digging at Midnight

Vijay had lived in Colombo for the last twelve years. He came to the South when he was but a boy of fifteen from his home on the Northern Shores of the Island. His uncle from his mother's side was a trader and brought him down to see the wonders of the big city. Vijay was immediately enamoured by the large buildings, many roadways, the countless number of vehicles and hordes of people that dotted the metropolis, and begged his uncle from his mother's side to let him stay on. He worked in his uncle's establishment and as time went by he grew older in years and wiser in mind and decided he would start a little business venture of his own. He had acquired the sharp acumen needed for executing business deals, and had made numerous friends whilst working for his Amiable Uncle. He made it a point of befriending those whom he believed could be of some help to him when the need arose, and therefore had built up quite an admirable accumulation of powerful associates. One of these was a Police Sergeant who used to visit the Shop. Vijay took it upon himself to attend to the Sergeant personally.

Some years later his Amiable Uncle decided to close up his business down in the South and return to his homeland up North. The time had come for Vijay to seek for himself. He contacted the Police Sergeant, who, by now, Fate had placed in charge of one of the suburban Police Stations. So he was now an Officer in Charge. Not an unsuitable title for a man who worked hard at his job and strove diligently to rise in his profession.

The OIC arranged for Vijay to get one of the many little shops which were being allotted to those interested, and as Fate would once again have it, these were located just by the Police Station. Vijay was most grateful to the Worthy Inspector and set about establishing a little grocery store in this place. But he had a problem in that he had no place to stay. He could not live in the shop as the space was just enough for himself and his groceries and so he was compelled once again to seek the assistance of his friend the Worthy Inspector to find him a suitable dwelling place.

The Worthy Inspector of course was a man of magnanimous nature and eager to help an Enterprising Lad, sought the help of the Chief Priest of the Big Temple which was situated on one side of the Police Station. The Chief Priest being kind and generous, granted permission most readily and willingly for Vijay to rent out one of the rooms on the Temple premises.

So Vijay was, as they say, set in life. He had a pleasant happy go lucky disposition and soon made friends with all those who visited the Temple as well. He never forgot to visit the Officer in Charge and always took him some little gift, a packet of pappadams or a few eggs, from the Grocery Shop, to show him how grateful he was for what the Worthy Inspector had done for him.

Time went by, as it was wont to do, and Vijay grew to be acutely aware of rumblings between his people in the North and those in the South. He absorbed with great interest all the gossip which spilt out at his Grocery Shop, listened to the radio and watched the television daily, in order to glean as much information as he could on the vital topic of the day.

He was disturbed at the pernicious turn of events between his People and those in the South, and decided to pay a visit to his Home so that he could get a more accurate perspective of the situation. While in the North, he made the acquaintance of certain Striped Felines who convinced him that they were on a Special Mission to save their Motherland - meaning of course the territory they claimed to be their own. Needless to say, Vijay was sorely tempted to stay on and join the Special Mission, but he thought of all the hard work he had put into his Grocery Shop and found it extremely hard to close it down and give up the life he had been now used to for so many years. The Striped Felines were most understanding and realised that the Clever Vijay should not be made unhappy; they consoled him by saying that there were many things he could do for the Mission even if he decided to stay back in the South. So, after much consultation and deliberation, he came back to the Temple and his little room and started work again at his Grocery Shop. All his friends were happy to have him back and greeted him with unparalleled joy.

Vijay was now not only Clever and Friendly, but had also become quite Wily and Wilful in his attitudes. The latter side of him he kept strictly within the portals of himself, and divulged his knowledge or plans to no one. The Striped Cats visited him often but in guises so varied and diverse that no one but Wily Vijay would have known that underneath their external attire they wore broad black stripes and their human masks covered their feline faces.

So life, as they say, went on. The Wily and Wilful Vijay had now become an expert at gathering intelligence needed by his Feline Superiors. They rewarded him handsomely for information on the movements of the

Police. Soon his Bank Balance in his Northern Home grew to proportions he never dreamed he would ever afford. His Grocery Shop was doing a booming business.

Meanwhile, in the Big City the Slick Striped Prowlers were creating Chaos and Havoc. Bombs were going off like fire crackers during festival time, and people were being exterminated like flies. Vijay read the daily newspapers and never failed to cut out items about these incidents, which he pasted in a scrapbook he had bought specially for this purpose. The Striped Boss ordered that he be given a cellular telephone so that he could be contacted conveniently. So it was not unusual to see Vijay with this modern mobile contraption glued to his ear - in earnest conversation with some High Up or Another among his Feline Bosses. Once again, as Fate would have it, on the other side of the Temple was the Army Camp. In fact, from the window of his room Vijay had a fair view of the entrance to the Camp. If he could have some elevation he knew he would get even a better view. So he suggested to the Priest that he wanted to build another floor over his room - a donation from him. The Priest, touched by his gratitude, accepted this gesture, and soon Vijay's little room had an upstair sit-out which in reality was not merely a sit-out but more so a look-out. He would sit there listening to his radio and through his powerful binoculars observe the movements at the Army Camp opposite him.

The Worthy Police Inspector paid him a visit one day, just when he was in the process of taking a look through his binos (as he called them).

"What are you looking at Vijay?" asked the Inspector.

"At birds sir, I like birds very much sir."

"An ornithologist! But I never knew!" the Inspector sounded surprised."So what can you see?"

"Brown coloured birds sir - many of them."

"What are they doing Vijay?"

"They seem to be - er - marching sir." replied Vijay, an element of veracity in his answer.

"Really? How extraordinary!" remarked the Inspector.

He came down and met the Inspector.

The Inspector wanted to come into his room, but Vijay did not want him to. Why only today a Sriped Cat brought in some "stuff" for him to keep. They were in his room, and he did not want the Inspector, or for that matter anybody, to see that. He had to find a suitable hiding place for all the stuff.

He told the Inspector he had to go out, and they walked out together, after Vijay had locked his room securely. Later that evening, he brought some banana saplings from his friend across the road. He asked the Priest whether he could use the mammoty which belonged to the Temple to dig a hole to plant these saplings. Sunil, the boy who cleaned the Temple premises, offered to help him. So together they dug a deep pit.

"Isn't this enough?" asked Sunil. "After all they are rather small saplings."

Vijay looked at the pit.

"Yes Sunil, that's enough- even if they look small, when you put them inside the pit they will grow large."

Sunil could not fathom this reasoning, but said nothing, as he felt that Vijay's knowledge in these matters was far greater than his.

Darkness settled on the Big City. It was a starless night. The silver moon wafted from behind one cloud to another. At midnight Vijay took his little treasure out from the box, and looked at them in the silence of the night and the safety of his room. Ten rifles, six hand grenades and- what were these? Why plastic dolls with explosives fitted inside their bulging stomachs! He looked at them in fascination. He covered them with a hessian bag, and wrapped them in several thick layers of plastic sheeting, and very gingerly carried them out to the compound behind his room. A dog barked and he stopped in his tracks. Fortunately it was only Tokka, the Temple dog who slept near his room. He wagged his tail and greeted Vijay, who gave him a pat on his head and moved on. Placing the cache at the bottom of the pit Vijay quickly covered it with soil. He had covered most of it when a sound made him spin around. In the faint light of the moon he saw Sunil.

"Aney - what are you doing at this time of the night! I heard a noise from this side and thought some hora had come no. What's this?" exclaimed Sunil.

For a moment Vijay's heart stopped beating. I have to be calm, he thought. "I was just planting the saplings" replied Vijay pointing to the banana plants which were lying beside the pit.

"But why are you doing this in the middle of the night - when everyone is sleeping?" asked Sunil passing him the saplings one by one.

"Why? It is because everyone is sleeping that I can plant these without being disturbed - during the day there is always some disturbance or another. Also when you plant these in the night they grow better." Vijay replied with a regained confidence.

Sunil though puzzled at this information thought it best to refrain from making any comment.

"I am going back to sleep" he sighed, leaving Wily Vijay to finish off filling up the pit with soil.

In the morning the Chief Priest was pleased to see the banana saplings looking so bright and sprouting from the plot of land next to Vijay's room. He was impressed with the hard work Vijay was putting into this project.

The administrators of the Feline Fiends were also very pleased indeed with their Man in Colombo. He was proving to be more useful than they had anticipated. They had successfully carried out many missions on behalf of their Movement in the Big City. The most recent was a massive bomb which had destroyed almost the entire business area in the Metropolis. This had been one of their most successful attempts at disrupting the economic stability in the country.

Security had tightened a hundredfold. The Police were making routine searches of specific areas on a regular basis. Civilians were asked to be vigilant and report any unusual activities and also to investigate any unfamiliar faces in their areas. Vijay found that he was often stopped at the checkpoints in the city, while he was going from one place to another.

Vijay felt it was time for him to move out. He informed his Feline Bosses about the situation he was faced with. They instructed him to move the cache to an address they provided, and then they would teach him their special Disappearing Act.

It was a difficult task for him to remove his little treasure from underneath the now well grown banana trees. He went to the Chief Priest and said "I need the mammoty again. I want to dig around the banana trees so that I can spread the fertiliser deep into the soil." So saying he raised up the bag of Special AK47 Banana Fertiliser he had with him. Sunil joined the conversation and was, as usual, ready to help him with his projects!

"Vijay, are we going to dig in the night again? That was really exciting to be out here digging while everyone was asleep!" Sunil was thrilled by the prospect of a midnight adventure. That very night Sunil and Vijay dug around the banana trees. The trenches became deeper and deeper. They spread the fertiliser in the drains around the tree.

When they came to the cornermost tree, Vijay said "Sunil you can go to sleep machang. I will finish this last one off. You have to get up early to sweep the place also, so you better have a good night's rest." Sunil was in fact thankful to get away. They had been labouring for almost two hours and the novelty of the whole thing had worn out. He was quite tired and badly wanted to get back to his mat and sleep.

Vijay waited until he was safely out of the area and dug deeper on the side of the drain in the corner. He felt the thud of the mammoty against his treasure. Carefully removing the soil with his hands, as he did not want to damage the important package, he unearthed the cache of arms he had hidden some weeks ago. He took the parcel to his room and placed it underneath his bed. Then he got back to the pit and covered it up.

Early the next morning he called his Striped Boss and was told where exactly to deposit the cache. He was just getting ready to go to his shop when he heard the sound of a police jeep inside the temple premises. The Worthy Inspector was talking to the Priest. They were looking in his direction. Vijay's jaws tightened. He felt there was something afoot - but he was ready to face the threat. If the worst came to the worst, he had the little silver capsule hidden in an inner pocket of his shirt. He would never get caught and betray his Masters. He would face anything for the sake of the Cause of the Striped Cats. He walked towards the Inspector and the Priest.

"Ah hullo Vijay - so how are you?" the Inspector greeted him.

"I'm alright sir." Vijay answered humbly.

"We are searching the whole area - we have arrested many suspects of the Striped Cat Movement" the Inspector said.

"Is that so Sir?" Vijay replied his voice lowered.

The Priest looked uncomfortable. He kept rubbing the palms of his hands against each other. They stood together for a moment in silence.

"Damn nuisance these Tigers - causing so many problems." muttered the Inspector.

Vijay looked at his watch. "Please excuse me Sir - have to go to the shop now." he said hurrying away.

Vijay knew his moment had come. Immediately he got to his shop he gave a call to his Feline Boss. He thought he recognized one of the policemen, dressed in ordinary clothes and reading a newspaper, sitting opposite his shop. His Feline Boss gave him an address. Vijay left from the back door of his shop. He walked down a muddy lane past some shanty houses and met his Feline Friend at the corner. A white van was parked under a tree. He got into it and his friend drove. His friend now passed him his new ID card. His name was registered as Mahen. They drove for over two hours and reached a house late afternoon. Vijay was now transferred to another vehicle which whisked him away. There were many checkpoints on the way but he had no problem with his new identity card. After many many hours of travelling he realised he was in his Homeland. There was nothing to worry about.

Meanwhile, the Inspector in the City down South was at Vijay's shop. He could not find him there. The boy who assisted him said he must have gone back to his room. The Inspector then went to the Temple, but the Priest had not seen Vijay. Neither had Sunil. The room was locked from the outside. They broke open the door and entered Vijay's room. The contents in the hessian bag and the pictures in the scrapbook were ample evidence that Vijay was in the Movement of the Striped Cats. The Inspector was shocked beyond words. The Priest was dumbfounded. Only Sunil managed to speak. "Aiyo - he has dug the last banana tree out completely!".

The Inspector and the Priest just looked at each other as the truth sank slowly in to their heads.

Nude with a Violin

Dudley Thotagama looked at himself in the mirror. He raised his shoulders and pushed out his chest, then drew in his stomach. My what an impressive figure I make, he thought. But it was only for a few seconds that he managed to maintain this stance, for the moment he exhaled, he turned into the flabby paunchy person he really was. He sighed as he brushed his hair, peering at his reflection. Oh the grey is beginning to show again, time I had another dye with that lovely lady hairdresser. He twisted his mouth as he combed his moustache with a tiny fine toothed comb and sprayed himself with a mist of after shave lotion. His wife Elisa was downstairs in the kitchen. Hmm he thought, that's her department. The kitchen and the house. Pity they didn't have any children then she would have had more to do. A woman's domain. He chuckled. His plantations were doing well and now with his government connections, there was a possibility of his being offered an ambassadorship. His eyes twinkled and he smiled to himself. He had always had the entrepreneur spirit in him and was a leader even while in school. As a young man there were many proposals for him. After all, he was a good catch, as they said, and it was after much consideration that he settled for Elisa. She came from a wealthy family of land owners in the central part of the Island. Her provincial upbringing and her quiet gentle manner suited him. He didn't want anyone too sophisticated or qualified - all these women who studied in universities and went abroad were dangerous in the long run. And the ones who lived in the city were too flashy and bold. They had too many ideas rolling around in their little heads and were too outspoken and independent for his taste. Elisa was just right. She was the ideal wife, stayed at home and looked after all the domestic affairs - servants, garden, meals, while he concentrated on the more important issues in life. She dressed modestly and her clothes were - he crinkled his nose while thinking of the word, ah yes -old fashioned and somewhat dull, quite unlike those worn by the fashionable crowd he met. Dudley enjoyed moving with the highest social circles - he loved nothing more than entertaining friends and well known personalities at his house. Although Elisa was not a lively socialite, he had to admit that she was an excellent organiser. The dinner parties and the luncheon get- togethers at their rambling house moved with professional smoothness - everything was always in place and the food was unquestionably scrumptious. Elisa didn't always sit with them but that didn't bother him, she was so quiet that her presence made no difference anyway. His friends remarked what splendid lunches and dinners he gave, and he smiled and nodded and took a deep breath of satisfaction, pleased at how well he had done for himself.

Tonight he was having the Minister of Foreign Affairs and some other government and private sector dignitaries to dinner - just a small gathering of about ten. They were to arrive at eight and now that it was a quarter past, he had dressed and was walking down the stairs when he heard Elisa already greeting someone at the door. As he went out to meet his visitors he was startled to see her dressed in a long slim black skirt and cream silk shirt. What's this? Why isn't she in a sari? She should have worn a sari - especially as the Foreign Affairs Minister and his wife were present. He frowned making a mental note to speak to her about this, although it would have to be after the party, as more people began coming in. There were some ladies also present and Elisa spoke briefly to them while she wove her way in between the groups seeing that they all had their drinks and the little nibbles she had arranged for them to have before dinner. Dudley sat next to the Foreign Minister's wife, a big blustery woman decked with gold bangles, necklace and large earrings and an Indian silk sari, who talked in a loud voice on subjects varying from pot plants to the Israeli-Palestinian crisis. The Foreign Minister himself was a slightly built man who spoke very little, and had to be prodded into giving his opinions about world affairs. Now that's the way a woman should dress, thought Dudley fixing his gaze on Mrs Foreign Minister. Stylish and shows her class - her wealth. I wonder what Elisa has done with all that jewellery I give her from time to time? Those silly little costume pieces she was wearing today looked so ridiculous. I really must have a serious word with her about this. After the guests had left Dudley smoked his last fine cigar - how they all appreciated the imported cigars he'd served them. He smiled to himself as he finished off his final glass of brandy while reflecting on the evening's events. Yes the conversation had gone off well and the FM did drop a hint about the proposed ambassadorship. If only Elisa had dressed with more decorum it would have made a better impression. He stubbed his cigar firmly into the ashtray. I'll speak to her about it right away. Noticing that her room light was on, he stopped by her door and gave it a few sharp raps. She opened it after a few moments and to his astonishment he found her dressed in a kind of shirt - it looked like a man's shirt at that, which reached just below her knee and to his greater surprise she had a paint brush in her hand. - "What the devil are you doing? Wearing this odd thing and carrying a paint brush in the middle of the night?"

She looked down at herself. "Why what's wrong? This is my night shirt and I'm in the middle of painting a picture."

Where were the chaste long flowing nightdresses she used to wear? She looked so - so absurd in this- quite indecent in fact. He noticed an easel set up near the window but it was backing him so he couldn't see the canvas. Dudley pursed his lips and looked around at the bright lights. "Electricity is very expensive - and you should do this in the morning."

"I have a class in the morning." she didn't look up from the picture she was painting.

"What class?"

She laughed - "Painting class."

He was piqued at her nonchalant attitude. This is what happens when you give them too much - I should never have given her a car and a driver, now she's gallivanting all over the place.

"Elisa - you should've worn a sari - why did you wear that skirt and that cheap jewellery- you knew that the Foreign Minister and his wife were coming."

She looked long and hard at him. "Why -what's wrong with what I wore?" She pursed her lips and went back to the easel.

"A sari would have been more in keeping with the occasion - with the Foreign -"

She guffawed. "And when did I dress to please the Foreign minister - such nonsense!"

He stood there for a few moments clasping and unclasping his hands.

"So - so what's all this?" he asked - waving his hand around the room.

"It's stuff for the exhibition - I've plenty to do."

"Exhibition? But you never told me?"

She ignored his comment and began putting her painting things away."I'm telling you now. Goodnight Dudley." she opened the door for him.

He stormed into his bedroom and paced the floor for a good ten minutes. "Insolent woman - I'll show her who's boss around here." He suddenly felt like having a drink. He rang the bell over his dresser and the houseboy appeared like magic at the door. "Piyasoma - bring the bottle of whiskey and a glass from downstairs -at once ." He sat on the lounge near the window and poured himself a drink. "Thinks she can get away with all this damn nonsense, I'll put her in her place." he muttered to himself.

Dudley had a luncheon at his Club the next day. He met with the American Ambassador and a host of ex pats - all holding high positions either in government connected projects or multi national ones which were based in Sri Lanka. Some of them were accompanied by their wives. Dudley didn't even mention the event to Elisa. She was useless at this sort of function anyway. But a troubled twinge pricked his mind as he thought of the previous night's incident. This painting nonsense must be some silly past-time that she and her friends were doing together. The way she spoke of an exhibition - such a pompous word - in all probability it must be some insignificant gathering for her old school friends. No she was really a home bird- this was just a passing phase.

When he returned home late that evening Elisa's room light was on again - he saw it as soon as he turned in through the gate. Painting again? This was going too far - he had to stop this nonsense. His electricity bill was staggering and there she was with the lights on late into the night - wasting it on some worthless hobby she had taken up.

He knocked on the door.

"Who is it" Elisa asked.

"Me - who else."

She opened the door after a few moments. Her room was in a mess. There were paintings all over and boxes and bags.

"What's this?"

"I'm packing my stuff for the exhibition - it's tomorrow."

Once again she was dressed in a short night shift and her hair was bundled up in a knot. He held his breath. Why she looked different from the Elisa he'd married - she looked like one of those fast women he met on his social rounds. The ones he had lunch and dinner with sometimes. He squirmed at the sight of her and felt quite dizzy. He left quickly before he lost control of his senses. But Dudley couldn't fall asleep. He tossed and turned in his bed wondering what had come over Elisa. Finally he took a sleeping tablet and managed to doze off.

The newspaper was always on the dining table when he came down for breakfast but today it wasn't there. He glanced at his watch - what had happened to the damn paper? Piyasoma was smiling when he brought it in almost fifteen minutes later.

"Ah Mahathayaya, very good no? Lady's picture in front page for winning art prize."

"What?" He was surprised to see that indeed Elisa's picture was on the front page accepting a prize for her picture of the Nude with the Violin. He couldn't take his eyes off the picture. Nude with the violin - from where the hell was that? Imagine his wife painting a nude with a violin? Couldn't she have done a violin on its own - and who the hell was the nude anyway? Suddenly he began to feel hot around the neck and sweaty under his arms. My God this is the limit - she's really got completely out of hand. I've been far too kind and generous to her, that's what. She's changed these past few months- like the way she came down to breakfast the other day in a pair of tight jeans and tee shirt.   His mother would have called her cheap. A cheap woman, that's what she'd become. That word cheap - it rang of fast females who lured innocent men into their clutches. Again the women he often spent time with came into his mind. In the photo she was wearing a pair of trousers and a loose shirt. What's happened to this woman? She's in bad company I know - I have to pull her out. Imagine her picture in the papers - all my friends will see it. The mere thought of it made him cringe. Damn! it could be so embarrassing for him - especially now with the ambassadorship floating on the horizon.

He rang the little bell on the table, specially placed there in case he wanted to summon someone in the house. Piyasoma appeared like the genie of the lamp.

"Tell Madam to come down - I want to speak to her."

"Madam gone out Sir."

"Gone out? Where?" Now where had she disappeared - and without telling him a thing.

"Gone for art class Sir."

"Art class?" My God this had to be stopped. This woman now lived at the art class. Even though he hadn't seen the picture, he visualised what the nude with the violin must've been like. Did the nude have the violin on his shoulder or what? Maybe he was standing behind the violin. He cursed under his breath.

"We are having guests tonight - does Madam know?"

"Madam has given all the instructions to the kitchen, Sir, she has made the two salads and also the two puddings to be served for dessert and put them in the fridge."

Well at least she had performed her duties.

Just at that moment a bright red sports car drove into the porch. A woman alighted, and from where he sat Dudley could make out a pair of shorts and shapely fair legs. She came running up the steps. He was unable to utter a word when he saw that it was Elisa - dressed in these revealing, these indecent clothes. She smiled becomingly at him.

"Oh Dudley, there you are. Good thing I met you because I may not be at the dinner tonight - but,"she raised her hand to stop his protests, "but I have organised everything - even the puddings."

Dudley felt his head about to burst and his heart thumped hard against his flabby chest.

"But - how dare you leave like this - it's your duty to stay here and look after our guests."

He found himself talking to no one as Elisa had already slipped away from him.

That evening Dudley spent more time dressing up than ever before. His mind was preoccupied with the antics of Elisa. She was behaving completely out of character. She was losing her sense of propriety. Didn't she realise that she had to maintain a certain status being married to him.

He was on his way downstairs when Piyasoma gave him a note.

"Lady said to give this Sir."

'Dear Dudley,' it read, 'I have gone with my Art Group to Bentota to celebrate my prize - I didn't think you'd want to waste your time coming as you were having guests to dinner. Hope the party goes off well. I've organised everything. Shall be back tomorrow evening. E'

Bentota - she had actually had the gumption to take off with her - her art group to Bentota.

What was he going to tell his guests if they should ask where she was? A headache, in bed with the flu - anything but the truth, he thought. He began to feel a slight dizziness come over him. The doorbell chimed signalling the arrival of the first guests.

"Ah-ha now your wife is a famous artist ah!"was the opening comment.

"Oh wonderful for Elisa to win the Art prize for the Nude with the Violin!" someone said to him.

"Oh yes, yes." he smiled, gritting his teeth.

"Such a virile nude." someone tittered. "Where did she meet him?"

The topic of conversation was Elisa and the art exhibition. Dudley hadn't gone to it but was too embarrassed to say so - after all it was his wife's exhibition, so he pretended he had been there.

"Oh yes - wonderful wonderful."

"By the way, where is Elisa?"

"Oh she's resting - a touch of the flu I think - nothing serious."

The night wore on and Dudley had a nagging headache by the time the last guest left.

After they'd gone he stalked up to Elisa's room and flung open the door. His eye went directly to the paintings stacked up against the walls. He marched up to them. I must have a look at this damn picture - nude with a violin indeed. But they were all scenes he looked at - sea scapes, landscapes, -all looking serene and quiet.

She has to stop this rubbish at once. I'll just ask her to leave, get out, and I won't give her a cent, no house, no land, no nothing. Teach her a good lesson on how to behave herself. I'll go to the bank and freeze her account and ask them to seal the jewellery in case she tries to take it away.

Next morning he met the Bank Manager who eyed him quizzically when he told him the story.

"Ah but she has already taken her jewellery and money out. She has in fact withdrawn the money from the joint account."

Dudley felt a strange numbness come over him. He gripped the arms of his chair with such force that his fingers stung. Of all the diabolical tricks!

"But she can't do this to me?" he blurted.

"She's done nothing to you - both the money and jewellery are legally hers - so there's nothing illegal about what she's done."

"But to do it without telling me a word about it? Isn't that dishonest and deceitful?"

The Bank Manager remained silent for a few moments. "Weren't you going to do the same thing to her?"

'Ah - but that's different, I am her husband and have a right to do this - whereas she- she's just a woman." his voice faltered.

He dared not go to the office, there might be some talk about the exhibition and he would go berserk if they even so much as mentioned the word art to him. Right now he needed a stiff drink.

"Gunadasa go straight home," he said to his driver.

Pot of Gold

Somawathie and Siripala were quite excited, for today their only child Geetha was returning from Dubai. Geetha had spent the last two years working as a housemaid there. Somawathie woke up early and boiled a kettle of water to make some tea for them before they went to collect her. Siripala hired a van to take them to the airport, as his elder daughter Dayawathie and her family of four, plus Somawathie's mother and younger sister and Siripala's brother were all going to welcome Geetha back home.

Somawathie remembered how sad she had been when her daughter left. She recalled with clarity how Geetha in her flower printed skirt and pale silk blouse, her feet shod in plain black slippers and her cascading hair braided into a plait which hung below her waist - walked into the inner depths of the Airport and then disappeared from sight for two whole years! And now she was coming back. It was wonderful!

Some mumblings on the loudspeaker system indicated that the plane had landed. Siripala was looking forward to seeing his "chooti duwa" as he called Geetha. Her innocent looks had made him want to protect her and he was shattered when she had decided to go on her own to work in some foreign country so far away. Anyway, now he could breathe with relief - for in a moment she would be here. They hovered at the railings, peering at the swing doors in front of them with eager concentration. Each time the doors flew open with their characteristic clicking sound, they expected Geetha to appear.

Passengers poured out through the doors like ants from an anthill. The doors opened and an enormous cardboard box emerged balancing precariously on a trolley. It moved forward slowly and stopped in front of the railings. Then a young woman dressed in a figure hugging shiny silk slim skirt and blouse appeared from behind it. She wore white net stocking on her legs and her feet were shod in red high heeled shoes. Her hair was shoulder length and a part of it was tied up at the back with a brightly coloured slide. The make up on her face gave her a slightly ghostly appearance, especially as the whiteness of her face, rosy cheeks and bright red lips contrasted sharply with the rest of her dark brown complexion. She smiled widely and came towards Somawathie. With a start they realised that it was indeed no other than their beloved Geetha.

"Aney duwa how nice to see you," exclaimed Somawathie and clasped her to her chest. Siripala was more restrained. On seeing his "little girl" looking so different, Siripala plunged into a kind of daze which left him speechless. The rest of the group just stood by mesmerised by this stranger who stood before them. Geetha was the only one who was at ease as she greeted them with unbridled joy.

Geetha had two more trolleys which she extricated from the mysterious rooms behind the swing doors. These were piled high with cardboard boxes and outsize plastic bags filled to the brim with all manner of things. In fact they had to hire a separate van to transport the baggage.

As the days went by, cardboard boxes of various sizes and shapes piled up in the little front garden of Somawathie's house, to form a mountainous heap. Soon Somawathie's hall had a large refrigerator, a washing machine and a TV set lining an entire wall. The music set-up was placed on top of a low cupboard. The glass cabinet was filled to the brim with electric mixers and blenders. Large glass vases choked with brightly coloured artificial flowers adorned the tops of tables and any other space which was available. Geetha's friends and relations who visited gazed in awe upon this extensive display. They admired, no doubt with a tinge of envy, Geetha's ability to amass such a wide array of goods after her stint in Dubai.

The entire neighbourhood was intrigued at the change in the quiet homely girl they had known before. After a while however, they got used to it and seeing Geetha in her Dubai outfits, as they called it, walking past them became a commonplace experience for them.

Siripala and Somawathie discussed the future of their beloved daughter.

"Must find a good man for Geetha. High time she got married no?" said Siripala.

"Yes - now she is almost twenty four. One year more and she will be too old for the marriage market. So must do it soon." remarked Somawathie.

Dayawathie's son Chootie Malli told them he knew just the man for Geetha. He had a friend who owned the mini supermarket at the junction. Chootie Malli spoke to Somawathie and they arranged for a meeting. He told them Sunil was doing quite well financially with his shop. Also he had a large house outside Colombo and owned a coconut estate in Kurunegala. Between Somawathie and Chooti Malli, the horoscopes of the couple concerned were exchanged and examined in great detail. After much consideration, and seeking out the correct nakath times, a meeting was arranged between Geetha and Sunil.

The day had arrived. Somawathie was bustling around making all sorts of culinary delights to entertain the prospective groom. Dayawathie was also helping her - scraping coconut, washing the utensils and mixing this and that. Geetha was in her room trying out her Dubai outfits. She had her tape recorder playing her favourite Hindi song at full blast. She tried out several hairstyles and various hair ornaments.

At six o'clock Somawathie spotted Chootie Malli and his friend at the gate. They came inside and met Siripala who was seated on his haansi putuwa on the verandah. Somawathie ran inside and gave Geetha the news.

"But Duwa you must not come out and see him till 6.17 the nakath time - I will come and call you. Otherwise it will be bad luck."

Somawathie peeped at this scene from a side window which overlooked the verandah. She was very careful to move the curtain only that much, so that she could see the prospective groom. With one eye she observed that he was tall with good features. He wore a white sarong and checked shirt. Somawathie looked carefully to see whether he was wearing a gold watch and chain - the symbols of true wealth. But no, he wore neither. In fact he didn't even have a ring on his fingers. This was so disappointing. He didn't seem a good catch at all. She was furious with her nephew, trying to dupe them with some ordinary character for Geetha.

Somawathie huffed to herself before she went out to meet the guests.

Geetha smiled - the thought of going out in exactly three minutes and meeting her future husband sent a thrill down her spine!

She adjusted her gold embroidered seenimuttai pink sari. Her hair was loose - a few locks caught up in a gold ornamental hair clip. Her face was powdered so that her skin took on a different hue, her dark eyeliner made her eyes look larger. Her brightly painted lips gave her a daring look - reflecting her mood at that moment.

Six seventeen and Geetha walked out with a tray of sweetmeats and a drink. She went to where Sunil was seated and held it coyly out to him. Their eyes met and Sunil looked taken aback at the sight he encountered. Why, she looked like her face had been plastered with flour paste!

They said a few words to each other and then Geetha made her way back into the house.   After they had left Somawathie held a post mortem on the situation.

"Aiyo such a useless fellow - he wasn't even wearing a watch! Imagine coming to look at a bride dressed like that! I don't believe all these stories about him being rich and all that - must be Chootie Malli's imagination!"

Siripala tried to say something good about the prospective groom. "Seems quite a decent chap - knew his business matters very well."

"What's the use of being decent and not being able to dress properly!"

A few days later Somawathie announced "I have contacted a magul kapuwa called Dingiri Banda. He is supposed to be very good. He had found a nice rich man for Malini akka's daughter. Malini said she will take me there."

Siripala was very relieved. This whole business of Sunil was too much for him.

Shortly afterwards, Dingiri Banda was contacted.

"Aney nangi" he said to Somawathie, "I can easily find a good, rich man for your daughter, especially as she has been to Dubai and also Malini akka tells me she has brought back lots of nice things. Give me Geetha's horoscope and I will see what I can do. There is Upali - a rich garage owner who is looking for a wife, I will speak to him. He is a little old, about fifty, but what does that matter?"

The matter of finding a husband for Geetha was then in Dingiri Banda's hands.

A few weeks later Dingiri Banda brought them the news that the horoscopes matched well, and he had fixed a nakath day and time for Upali to visit Geetha. It was to be the following week. Once again, the household was bustling with preparations for the visit of yet another prospective bridegroom.

Endangered Species

Simon's old school friend Bolay was celebrating his sixtieth. Everyone we've spoken to has been invited – it's going to be one of those grand affairs.

"Oh you know - the Minister will be coming so it will be quite a posh thing." my friend Sumana informs me.

I pass on this titbit of information to Simon.

"Minister? From which church?"he asks.

"Not church men - a minister from the government."

"Ah - one of those." He shudders.

Sumana has got herself a new sari and is planning to have her hair specially styled for the occasion. According to her, most of the ladies will be doing the same. I listen silently to all this tittle tattle. Finally the great day arrives.   There is already a crowd when we get there. Simon is hastily taken to the men's side - a cluster of men some standing, some seated, all with glasses in their hands - drinking some 'strong stuff' arrack or whisky or whatever. I am trundled off to the ladies' side - a group of ladies are perched demurely in a circle, some talking, some just silent. The drinks are all 'soft' ones on this side - ginger beer, iced coffee, or cordial.

I look around for Sumana and spot her with a group of ladies seated at the far end of the hall. She is hardly recognizable in her new hairdo. Other than her, I don't seem to spot any familiar faces. I'll have to make friends with those in my group I reckon, so I turn to the lady on my right and smile. She just stares back. I meet her unblinking eye hesitantly.

"Are you a Kandyan?" she asks knitting her eyebrows.

"Er- no."

"Oh." she says in disbelief, "But you look like a Kandyan no."

I am taken aback. Then I realise my sarong and blouse and middle parted hair tied in a knot at the nape of my neck must be making me look like a Kandyan.

"What did you say your name was?" The eyebrows meet again.

I repeat my name very slowly."An-the-a."

"Ah -yes you can't be a Kandyan no, with that funny name."

I bristle. I love my name. I take pride in it. "Why what's so funny about it?" I spit the words out.

"It's not a Singhalese name no?"

"No no – it's really of Greek origin –"

She puts her hand over her mouth and laughs.

"Ha- Greek- you're from Greece then?"

"No - I'm a Sri Lankan -"

"From here?"

"Yes -I'm a Burgher - from here."

She squints. I can see the McDonald's burgers floating through her mind. Am I a cheese or chicken?

"A Burgher - you know? " I say, although I know she doesn't know.

"Ah -" She's trying to look smart but her nincompoopish look cannot be hidden. Not from this sharp Burgher eye anyway.

Another lady has now joined us. "I used to know a lot of Burghers aney - but that was those days - now of course there aren't any here no?"

I feel many pairs of eyes now focused on me. I am a unique creature - a lost culture - I have attained almost prehistoric importance now. Come on you Burgher - put on your best look, keep your shoulders down and don't hunch. Think of those intrepid Dutch conquerors, Rikjkloff van Goens, and Hulft, and van Angelbeek and whoever else- who came here, kicked out the Portuguese, grappled with the Sinhalese and finally threw their hands up when the Brits arrived. It was no point being aggressive I reckon, so I give them all a big smile. Show that you're friendly, a little voice tells me.

"Yes- most of my relations are abroad."

They continue to gawk at me and one of them says, "Sin no - you must be all alone then?"

"Well not exactly - I have a family you know."

"Ah really?" they sound surprised.

"Yes I'm married and have two children."

"You're married? To whom?" as though this was highly impossible.

I took a deep breath. "To that Sinhalese gentleman in the green shirt" I replied pointing to Simon who was looking quite happy slurping on his

Scotch.

"Sinhalese?"

"Hmm." I nod.

They continue to stare at me.

"So what was your name then - those days?"

"When I tell them." they look at each other and titter.

"My what's that name?"

"A Burgher name - like Bartholomeusz, and Gratiaen, and Leembruggen and Kriekenbeek and Van der Straaten -" the names leap out of my mouth like thunder from a Dutch cannon.

They giggle and gawk at me like I'm talking some gobbledegook.

"Aney - what kind of names are those? I have never heard those names no, are all these people living in Sri Lanka?"

A flurry of excitement prevents me from saying anything. Young men, hovering on the brink of boyhood, dressed in army fatigues and carrying guns, rush into the garden. They glance sideways and hold their weapons close to their bodies, ready to gun down anyone who acts even slightly suspicious in their eyes.

"He's come, he's come-" they gasp and everyone stands, the ladies adjust their saris and hairstyles and set their toothpaste ad smiles across their faces. We see the men on the verandah and the lawn leap to attention. I stand because everyone else does.

"Who's come?" I whisper to the lady closest to me.

She gives me a look of disgust. "Why the minister no!" I should've known.

The Minister who is a small angular sort of chap struts in with great gusto, trailed by a band of bodyguards and followers. He is dressed in a flowing off-white shirt and sarong, his dyed hair sleekly combed forward to hide an obvious bald patch. Two young boys dressed in designer shirts and pants and sporting the latest hairstyles stomp behind him, also carrying guns.

"Who are those?" I ask.

"They're his sons no," someone hisses in my ear, unwilling to talk too loud and interrupt the proceedings.

"Sons with guns?"

"Shhh."

What next? I thought. Daughters with mortars, wives with knives? The Minister and his entourage are directed to some inner room by our host. They disappear from sight and we return to our seats.

About half an hour later our hostess flitters across to us, her seeni-muttai sari fluttering on her ample shoulder. "Come aney for dinner – the minister is also serving, so come before the men come and take over." She giggles as she totters off to another group of ladies to pass on this vital information. We walk towards the dining room. The minister is still at the table. His plate seems to have disappeared under the mound of food he has served himself. A bodyguard dashes forward to carry his invisible plate, and follows the minister towards a table laid out specially for him and some other VIPs. We meander past the food and serve ourselves. There are stringhoppers, pittu, vegetable rice and all manner of curries - chicken, beef, seer fish, fried prawns, polos mallung, achcharu plus a host of other mouth watering delicacies. An old amme and a young boy are busily making appa on one side of the room, and we stand in line to collect the egg hoppers and plain ones.

The minister has a voice which belies his stature. When he speaks, it bounces like a rubber ball, right across the room.

"Damn shame about the war - that's what's ruining the country," he declares, "Those Tamils should all go back to India and leave this place to us. After all, we are the real people of this country." he stabs his chest with his fingers several times as he speaks, flashing his gold rings and the gold Rolex on his wrist. "Now see, our culture is so ancient, it is our pride and strength." With this statement he rams a fistful of food into his mouth.

There is a hushed silence – all eyes are on him as he chews and chews and chews.

Then -"Yes - our culture —our two thousand years of history can never be compared to anything else."

Our host agrees wholeheartedly, nodding his head with every word he speaks. Some of the ladies are riveted. They stop serving their food, mesmerized by the minister and his group. The sons have laid down the guns and are indulging in some drinks with the host.

"Yes - now see the Americans - they have no culture at all – what, only four hundred years no - and all the riff-raff from England went there."

"Worse in Australia no - all the English convicts went there. Imagine!" another voice breaks in.

"We are of course a pure race - full of history- no culture to beat ours onething, two thousand years – imagine - ha!"

The riveted ladies continue to gaze at the minister in awe. They try to catch his eye and then give him a smile, so that later they can boast to their home people and friends, "My the minister smiled at me aney!"

We then move back to our seats, where with our plates of food balanced precariously on our laps, the ladies continue the trend of the conversation we have just heard.

"Aney yes - we have so much of traditions - not like these other people. And we are so hospitable - not like those foreigners."

"Those foreigners are very shallow - not like our people. Our people are of course so good no."

Our people I wonder - who on earth are they? These hospitable lovers of humanity who are fighting one another and killing each other to boot, with their customs and traditions and smiles and what have you. An icy draft suddenly catches me, making me shiver. I am also "our people" but on the rim, on the perimeter. I don't have thousands of years of culture pressing down on my shoulders. I am a Burgher, with a funny first name and a funny surname, a left over from some colonial past long forgotten I belong to a minority in this country - not really to be taken seriously or considered as part of the population. Suddenly, I feel quite strange - a kind of not being here feeling. I have floated out of the room, out of the conversation. Like some people who die, I experience the bizarre sensation of leaving my body. I hover over the dining table, and listen to this and that -a strange lonely sense of not belonging comes over me.

I am jolted back into reality.

"Do you work?" This question always baffles me. What does it mean? Do I work in the house - meaning house-work, or do I do a job to earn money - or what?

It's too complicated to tell them the things I do - my kind of work; studying for some exam, writing articles for magazines and stories for workshops, painting pictures, quilting - all sound some sort of therapy for psychotic cases. At this point I am ready to scream, but I know I mustn't lose my cool. My status must be maintained at any cost.

"Yes." I reply boldly.

"Where?"

"At the Dutch Museum and the National Museum" I am determined to keep the Dutch ancestors in focus through all this Lion talk I've been subjected to.

"True ah? What do you do there?"

"I stand in the showcase which displays the Burghers - two days at one place and two days at the other."

"Aney really?"

"It's quite fun - though tiring - lots of people come and look at me - I'm a rare species you know - on the endangered list, only found in museums these days."

They look open mouthed. Now I had really become a unique specimen in their midst. My kind has to be protected.

But my moment of glory is short-lived. Everyone leaps to attention again – the Minister and his entourage are leaving. The sons stride past us, guns held aloft. We remain still, not even daring to breathe.

Time for me to leave too. I spot Simon and am about to walk towards him when the lady who first spoke to me places her hand on mine. "Soo nice to meet you. Still for all - can't say you're a Burgher! You look just like a Kandyan aney!"

The others with her also nod and smile in agreement. I press her hand and smile as I move away.

Handle with Care

In my opinion, Marcus was, to use a common cliche, a pain in the neck. He was young and pompous and strode around with an "I know it all" air that would put anyone with an ounce of sense completely off him. The thing was, he was a clever storyteller, and this drew people to him. It made him popular - though not exactly loved.

He had doting parents who believed he was God's own gift to humankind. His younger sister hung on every word he said, and followed him around somewhat like that foolish lamb did with Mary. She had that same wide wonder-eyed look that lambs have, especially when they are lost.

However, his parents were old family friends of ours, and I was compelled to put up with Marcus and his pretentious ways from time to time, when he came out on holiday from England.

He was seated on our little verandah, adjusting his glasses, his eyes dissecting every picture and ornament into shreds.

"So Marcus, how are Grissy and Sebastian?" I asked after his parents. I felt guilty that I hadn't kept in touch with them for over a year.

"Oh so-so." He replied.

"And Amanda?" - this was his lamb sister.

"So-so -"

"What do you mean 'so so' are they well or what?" I was exasperated.

"If you mean physically - I suppose you could say they were in trim shape - but mentally, well that's another story". I chose to ignore the latter remark.

He sipped the orange juice I had poured out for him, with a slow rolling of the liquid on his tongue - like wine tasters do. Then, he swallowed the juice with an abstract air on his face. He had a knack for making simple things seem complicated.

"How's your grandmother?" I asked for want of anything else to say.

"God knows". He replied callously, turning the glass in his hand.

"What do you mean?" My patience was being tried to its utmost and my voice had reached some semitones higher even to my ears.

"Don't you know about Grandmother?" He asked curiously, as though I was hiding something from him.

"Know what?" I said.

"Well" he sighed "It's a long story."

Last summer they had holidayed in France, where some friends owned a vineyard, he started to relate.

"We ought to take mother with us" said Sebastian. "She's old and needs some fresh country air - will do her loads of good." He stood with his hands in his pockets breathing in deeply as though he were standing right in the middle of some French vineyard, taking in the subtle aroma of the grapes - when he was actually inhaling the fumes of his pipe. He broke into a fit of coughing.

"Take grandmother with us!" exclaimed Marcus who was busy cleaning out his fish tank. He loved his fish - perhaps because they never objected to his company. He would ply them with his opinions and sayings and they would just swim along silently in their usual tedious manner - up and down, up and down - in the artificial blue surroundings of their container.

"Why not?" said Grissy, for once questioning her son's statements.

So it was settled. Grandmother would go with them to France. She would sit outside their chalet and gaze at the grapes and feast on the fresh unpolluted country air. At eighty five she was a wiry little lady. Although she was so small and fragile looking, her hot temper was the talk of the town. Why, it was only a few years back that in a fit of anger she threw a heavy wooden stool at the local parish priest, who was paying his monthly visit to her! Ever since, everyone kept her at arms length, and on her good side, in case they too were subjected to her wrath.

Soon they were packed and ready and were looking forward to their trip on newly opened Chunnel, Grandmother was most excited. She put away a bag full of biscuits and her favourite gin and orange juice, just in case they met with some breakdown and were stranded in the tunnel.

"Can't trust these modern things." She mumbled to herself.

Marcus was silent with his grandmother. Apart from her hearing being poor, he too respected her hot temper, so he remained mute in her company.

She was disappointed the Chunnel trip proved to be so normal. There were no breakdowns and no fires. "We might as well have come on the ferry," she complained.

They picked up the car they had rented at the French end, and proceeded to travel into the country to their vineyard. They stopped at a wayside restaurant "Chat N'oir" to have a bite before they reached their destination, Grandmother took her gin and orange juice inside with her and promptly poured herself a stiff drink.

"Need one after all that travelling." she said.

They settled for a light meal of croissants, mushroom omlettes and French bread. The delicious aroma of the food infused them with the holiday spirit. Soon they were drinking wine and laughing happily.

Grissy and Sebastian went on long walks, and Amanda became friends with the neighbours - which kept her busy. Marcus found to his utter disdain that most times he was left alone with Grandmother! What a bore! He hopped into the car and disappeared into the nearby village, which, to him, was as boring as his Grandmother. He found no one who was interested in him or his ideas and put it down to them being simple village folk who were far beneath his intellectual status. He roamed aimlessly from place to place, searching for something he could never seem to find.

That evening, at the dinner table, he declared his strong sense of boredom and his family paid close attention to his words. Grandmother just slurped on her soup, not even looking up as she didn't even know he had made any statement at all.

"I know what - let's drive across to Germany for a day or two - it's just a few hours away and we could experience something different. We could get back home from there". Declared Sebastian. So next day they woke up early and started on their trip.

Grandmother had a stiff shot before she left - "To take me through the journey" she declared,

As they drove by a river they gazed in awe at the ancient castles that stood on the mountainsides.

"Are we on the chunnel?" Asked Grandmother.

"No, we're driving past a river." replied Grissy.

"A river? Is it the Seine?"

"Grandmother," said Marcus, gaining confidence at her confusion, "we are in Germany."

"Germany? Oh dear all this time I thought we were in France. Sebastian you never told me we had vineyards in Germany - and all those fine houses too." she said, beaming at yet another castle they spotted.

They rented out some rooms at a small wayside hotel and stayed overnight.

Grissy and Sebastian shared a room. Amanda shared with Grandmother and Marcus was on his own. To Amanda's great consternation she could not sleep a wink because Grandmother's rumbling snores kept waking her up. So she moved into her parents' room in the middle of the night and slept on the couch there.

Next morning Grissy tapped on Grandmother's room door but there was no answer. Fortunately the door was not locked and she went inside. Grandmother was lying on the bed, her mouth half open as it usually was when she slept.

"Grandmother, wake up - we have to leave in a while" said Grissy gently shaking her shoulder.

But Grandmother was immobile. She did not stir a jot. In fact, Grandmother was dead.

Grissy was stunned. She gasped in shock and total disbelief.

"How could you do this to us Clara! Right in the middle of our holiday! she resorted to calling her by her first name - which she never did during her lifetime.

Grissy knew it was detrimental to tell Sebastian this news - he would probably just burst into tears and do nothing. Amanda was equally useless. Only her son, her Marcus, with his practical turn of mind could deal with this catastrophe, and so she proceeded down the corridor to his room.

"Oh no! " gasped Marcus. "Such a mess -and I had planned to tour some of the castles this afternoon. I'll have to cancel that I suppose." He sounded quite vexed.

"Do we tell the Police?" Asked Grissy.

"Police?" shrieked Marcus. "Mother you must be mad. Why they would want an autopsy, they might even think we murdered her and would probably take us all in as suspects - interrogations, reports and the works.

Can't you see, this must be kept absolutely secret ! We'll have to smuggle Grandmother out of the country."

"But we will have to tell your father and sister." Broached Grissy.

"Such a nuisance - but I suppose so". Grumbled Marcus.

Grissy tried to be as gentle as possible when she broke the news to Sebastian and Amanda. Sebastian as she predicted, just burst into tears.

"Oh mummy, mummy" he wailed, tears streaming down his ruddy face, soaking into his moustache.

Amanda was no better. She clutched onto her father and wailed "Oh daddy oh daddy". With tears streaming down her face. Fortunately she had no moustache to get soaked.

While this duo were in full play, Marcus and Grissy were sorting out Grandmother.

Marcus had the bright idea to turn her into a package. His imagination always took a wild turn in a crisis.

"We'll wrap her up in the strongest thickest brown paper and put her into the boot of the car - then we just drive across."

Grissy was somewhat disturbed at this suggestion, but not having any other ideas in mind, succumbed to his proposition.

Marcus visited the stationery shop just as they were opening up.

"Ah our first customer," greeted the owner.

"Yes - I would like the strongest thickest brown paper - several sheets" he asked.

They had just the thing he wanted. And to cap it all, there was "Fragile - Handle with Care" signs printed on it. It was literally "untearable" paper - some new fangled product.

"Is it something delicate that you are packing?" the owner asked.

"Well - yees - I guess so". Marcus, finding the questions quite disagreeable.

When he got back to the hotel, the rest of his family were gathered in Grandmother's room.

Sebastian was standing rock still as if he were mesmerised and Amanda stood equally motionless beside him. They looked like two statues. But anything was better than the wailing duet they had performed earlier.

Marcus and Grissy wrapped Clara in an extra blanket they discovered in one of the cupboards in her room. Her frail thin body resembled a bird, and her fragile limbs seemed as though they would snap into pieces. Then they put the heavy brown paper around her several times. Hardy sticky tape bound all the loose ends together. Now the question was to get her out of the hotel. They cleared all her things and packed them back into her little valise.

"Amanda - stand near the door and tell us should anyone come along the corridor," Marcus ordered.

Amanda snapped out of her hypnotic state and got into action. Almost robotic, one might say.

Grissy and Marcus lifted Grandmother in her paper wrapping and carried her to their room next door. She was much heavier than they expected her to be, and there was much heaving and ho-ing before they managed to get her into their room.

The bell boy came up to clear their bags.

"What's in this?" He said surveying the package. "Looks heavy"

Marcus was not to be perturbed.

"Come - let me help you get that down to the car." He said lifting it with the boy.

Grissy rushed down to settle the bill and also to divert the owner's attention that their party was now minus one individual. Marcus told the boy to get the other bags from the room, while he bundled Sebastian and Amanda into the back seat of the car - fearing that at any moment they might well break into their weeping act. They packed the bags into the boot, placing the package at the edge - nicely wedged in so that it would stay in one place. The extra parcel made it difficult to close the boot, but with some effort, Marcus managed to get it shut.

Marcus drove. Grissy sat beside him, and Sebastian mute and swollen eyed sat with Amenda in the back seat.

At the German border, they had to stop at the checkpoint.

"Ah, your papers," the officer requested.

Everything was in order.

Marcus started to drive off, when a loud "Halt!" Stopped him in his tracks.

Marcus went cold. Now what?

"Young man - the lock on your boot seems to be loose." the guard walked up to the car.

The boot had opened a trifle.

Marcus' knees quaked as he stepped out of the car.

The guard had opened the boot -"Too many bags zat's why it will not close properly". He laughed. "Hmm" said the officer, just running his hands over the bags - and grandmother packed up. "Zis iz the parcel that is sticking out." He remarked his hands on the paper package. "Zum beautiful German work of art no doubt - zo well packed?"

"Oh yes - we love German art it's a - its a -"

" Statue?"

"Ah yes - that's what it is, a statue"

He closed the boot, smiling in approval of Marcus' words of appreciation of German art.

Relieved, Marcus got back into the driving seat. If his hands trembled, he tried hard not to show it,

In a few hours they would be at the Chunnel entrance.

The "Chat N'oir" came into view. They were exhausted and strained from the recent events, and decided they should stop and have something to refresh themselves. They parked the car in a side alcove and walked to the Restaurant.

Almost an hour later, having eaten well and drunk some delectable wine they returned to the car. As they reversed they heard a "thump" sound from the rear. Marcus alighted and was astounded to find the boot lock completely removed - it had been broken into! He looked inside and was shocked beyond words to find that two of their bags containing clothes and the vital brown paper package had disappeared. Someone or some persons had unwittingly robbed his grandmother! The three other occupants of the car stood by the boot staring in stunned horror.

Now what were they supposed to do? Imagine going to the police and reporting "the loss of two bags and my grandmother who was wrapped up in brown paper, from the boot?" No it wouldn't do. They had no choice but to keep quiet about the incident and continue on their journey.

Sebastian and Amanda looked as though they were once again going to break into their duet, so Marcus hastily bundled them back into the car where they burst into a flood of weeping and wailing. Grissy sat with a grim look on her face. Marcus, for once in his life, was lost for words or thoughts. Now his hands visibly shook on the steering wheel.

They drove through the Chunnel and back to their cottage in Kent in absolute silence except for the bursts of weeping from the two at the back.

It took them quite some time for them to settle down to their daily routine.

When friends asked it how their Grandmother was, they said she was on holiday in France - staying with friends.

After some weeks they said she was critically ill. They had to pretend to rush down to France to see her. What they actually did was to drive down to Brighton and spend a few days by the sea.

They returned with the sad news that "poor grandmother had passed away," and they had decided to bury her in France. Notices were put in the local newspapers - deepest sympathies poured in from friends and relations.

"She was a great lady," remarked the local priest who had been at the receiving end of the wooden stool earlier on. Sebastian, who was an only child wept copiously. Their friends were very understanding and extended a great deal of sympathy towards him. I was quite shocked by the story. I didn't know whether to believe Marcus or not. He was such a weird boy, he would make up gory stories - even about his Grandmother - he was quite capable of it.

"Have to go" said Marcus, standing up and flicking an imaginary speck of dust off his well cut trouser. He was leaving that night.

I couldn't help chuckling as we said goodbye.

"What's so funny?" He asked.

"I was just thinking - what a dreadful fright it must have given those robbers. The sight of your grandmother as they unwrapped the 'package' must have sent them reeling!".

"Grandmother always loved shocking people anyway!" Marcus remarked in wicked delight.

Looking for Some Place

This can be a most tiresome task - looking for some place you have never been to before. Even if you are armed with details of number and street name, locating an unfamiliar destination can be quite frustrating. Like the other day, we set out to see a young friend of ours who had recently lost her mother. We felt we had to see her and offer what comfort and sympathy we could on her bereavement. The number of her house was 694, the name of the road was Kopiwatte and the place was Bandagama. Briefed with what we thought was shatterproof information, we set out on our altruistic mission.

I went with Lorni and her driver Velu. We set out at about three in the afternoon, just when the sun was at the level where it streamed into the car hitting us right between the eyes. Apart from loathing the sun falling on any part of me, this was the time of the day when I indulged in my afternoon siesta with my dog Julie snuggled beside me, but I decided to put up with all the discomfort in the name of duty and friendship and whatever other good and commendable cause I could think of.

So off we went. Chit-chatting along the way, we reached Bandagama in what seemed like no time at all. Now all we had to do was to find Kopiwatte Road and number 694. Simple. We got to a junction with not two or three, but five roads leading away from its centre roundabout! There was no name-board to any of these roads, so we had to stop and ask someone for directions. Velu rolled down the shutter really smoothly, like the mobster chiefs do in the movies, and spoke to a man who was standing right there on the roadside- as though he was waiting all his life for this special moment.

"Ah, Kopiwatte Road," repeated the man in a slow deliberate voice to Velu's query. "You can go this way, or that way, both those roads go to Kopiwatte road - I think." So saying he waved both arms in front of him embracing the entire countryside which lay before us.

We were confused, not knowing whether we should proceed on this road or that one. We decided to follow our noses and bravely take one of the roads. After about half an hour of travelling, we were still not sure where we were. So once again we stopped and asked. This time we spoke to a lady carrying an umbrella with two little children walking beside her. The fact that she was well protected against the scorching sun, made me certain she must have been intelligent enough to give us some useful information.

"Can you tell us where Kopiwatte Road is, please," I asked.

She looked hard at us. "You are on Kopiwatte Road," came the quick retort. I felt terribly foolish, but just nodded my head as if to say I had known this all along and was just checking.

Velu couldn't bear to be left out of this discussion. "Can you tell us where number 394 is?" he asked.

The lady continued to look hard at us. Then she pointed to a number on the nameboard of a wayside shop. "That is 111, so 394 must be further up," she explained very slowly. She looked quite nonplussed. "These people go in cars, but they cannot read it seems," she muttered to her children as we drove off.

We proceeded at a pace which would have kept all the snails and tortoises in the world at the front line.

"Why are you going so slowly?" Lorni asked Velu. A note of distinct irritation had crept into her voice.

"I am looking for the number lady. Ah this is 268, now there's 280 and then there is 45/2 and 95 and 101 - aney I don't know where this number is no lady!" Velu sounds desperate.

Lorni's patience was now wafer thin. "If you go so slowly, we will get there tomorrow!" she snapped.

Velu was quite undeterred. "Ah, here's 310 and 318 - my lady we must be very close to 394!" He wore a happy smile that at last he had found his goal.

"Isn't the number 694?" I asked meekly, not wanting to be a wet blanket to all these exciting discoveries.

"Is it?" asked Lorni, looking at me.

"Er - I 'm not sure," I stammered.

"If you are not sure, then why did you say it?" she retorted. Time to keep quiet, I thought.

"Ah here's number 725 - must be very close now no lady?" said Velu.

This was too much for Lorni. "Now see what you've done! We have passed 394 and have to turn back." she said, with annoyance pouring out of every syllable.

So we turned back. Velu stopped at a kade and asked where 394 was. The man just shrugged his shoulders. "What is the name of the person?" he queried.

Lorni answered, "Miss Peck."

Velu repeated, "The lady's name is Peck." The kade man looked bewildered.

"Pack? Pack?" he repeated, not knowing what to make of this strange name.

"Not Pack. Peck." Lorni screeched. The kade man looked positively peeved at Lorni's outburst.

"Ah then- why don't you go and ask from the Police Station?" he suggested smugly.

The Police Station was in the opposite direction. So we had to turn back again. There was a man walking on the road, and Velu felt compelled to ask him exactly where the Police Station was.

"The Police Station!" the man exclaimed in a loud voice. He peered into the car and took a good look at us. "Why, why do you want to go to the Police Station?" He spoke to Velu, but his eyes were on us.

Meanwhile there were some road workers nearby, and hearing the word "police" they too came rushing to see what this was all about.

They came up to the car and peered inside. Velu felt he had to give them a proper explanation. "Aiyo we have to find this lady whose mother died recently. Real sin aney! The lady is all alone now. The funeral was at Kanatte and these two missis went for it also. Real sin aney! We are trying to find number 394 but as nobody seems to know where it is, we thought we should ask at the Police Station."

The workers dispersed, disappointed in the anticlimax they had confronted. They pointed further up the road indicating where the Police Station was, just a few yards ahead.

"Why don't you write down the number on a piece of paper and give it to Velu to show the Police?" I suggest gently. "Why don't you give him that piece of paper from your bag."

Lorni delved into her handbag and pulled out a piece of paper. Then

101

in a slow voice she remarked. "Ah yes, the number is 694 - you were right." I feel quite pleased that I knew it all along!

Velu runs his comb through his hair and smoothens his shirt before he walks into the Police Station.

There are three policemen sitting outside. Two are reading the newspapers and the other is examining his finger nails. They all look up expectantly when Velu walks in. Perhaps this is their only arrest for the day, or week or even months! But no, he only wants to know about some number. They have never heard of the number. "The best thing." they say, "is to look at all the numbers on the boards as you go along - then you are sure to find it."

One of the policemen comes right up to the car with Velu. Lorni asks him where the Post Office is - perhaps they would know. Once again we move in the opposite direction. We pass the road workers and they look up in surprise, wondering whether we have nothing better to do than to keep driving up and down the road.

We drove on and on and almost half an hour later we came to a large plantation full of trees. We passed through large open wrought iron gates drinking in the cool shade of the beautiful trees that lined the road. After a while of driving through this scenic area, we realised that we were on someone's private property.

"We better turn back," Lorni sounds alarmed, "we might be arrested as tresspassers."

So for the umpteenth time, we turned around and drove back the way we came. Just as we got out of this estate, we came across the board we were searching for - there it was "Sub Post Office". The board was pointing downwards. Velu got out of the car and looked longingly at the board, perhaps it was an underground Post Office? Meanwhile, Lorni had got out and walked down the road. Then Velu looked upwards.

"Why are you looking up?" I asked.

"To see any white flags - if we can see white flags we can find the funeral house easily."

I didn't dare look up into the grizzling sun - let Velu discover the flags. My head was aching, and I decided to sit and wait for them in the car. I could see Lorni running across the road to a kade, and gesticulating with her hands. Then she went across the road again and disappeared into a little building which we discovered was the very Post Office we were looking for. She was talking to the lady behind the counter. Lorni came back to the car, her face was jambu red and she was spluttering something quite incomprehensible.

"They don't know anything at this place," she fumed.

We proceeded in absolute silence.

"We should ask at a house instead of stopping at these strange places and asking all these people on the road." Lorni says after a while.

"Yes," says Velu, never wanting to be left out of a situation. "They are all useless. Useless place this is, no flags or anything. They don't know where any number is. Such a sin also for that lady to live all by herself in a place like this!"

We passed a house with some boys standing in a group, talking, at the gate.

Lorni got out of the car, and so did Velu. So I also got down. My head was splitting but I had to show some enthusiasm about the whole thing.

"Can you tell us where number 694 is?"Lorni inquires.

"Such a sin aney, that lady's mother died only last week and the lady is all alone now." Velu is determined to give them a comprehensive picture.

"How did she die?" one of the boys asks.

"Ah - is she the one who fell into the well?" another pipes in excitedly.

Velu looks very uncomfortable now. "Er - I don't know how she died. Anyway, why are there no flags?" he asks, trying to change the topic.

"What flags?" asks a boys.

"White flags," replies Velu.

They all look upwards searching for the flags which are not there.

We have learned nothing new. Drained of all energy and enthusiasm we walked back to the car. Number 694 has proved to be more of a mystery than we ever dreamed of. Lorni looks grim and is silent, and Velu is mumbling under his breath. My head is spinning and I have decided to shut my mouth and my eyes and just sit tight.

"Well, if we can't find it, we can't find it," murmurs Lorni in a harassed tone.

I am quite pleased but do not say anything. At last we might get the joyful chance of going back home now!

We pass the roadworkers for the third time. They are just packing up to go home, and look more than surprised to see us yet again. They point at us and laugh.

"What are those chaps laughing at," says Lorni, sounding huffed. I just keep my mouth shut, as though I did not notice anything. I have to keep my mouth shut because I am having great difficulty stifling a giggle, which I manage very cleverly, to turn into a cough!

We slow down in the traffic and just by the car there is a lady standing by the gate of a house. The way Lorni looks at her, I know what she is thinking of. I sink further into my seat and decide I will just let my head split open here and now, and let my throbbing brain spill out all over the car and create one big mess.

Lorni is now talking to the lady and looks quite pleased with herself. So I decide to see what has taken place. I cannot believe that this lady actually knows our friend! She tells us that Miss Peck does not stay at 694 anyway. Oh what a revelation! She gives us a new address which, according to Lorni, seems quite simple to find. By now I have lost all interest. The lady has also told Lorni that our friend was going for a prayer meeting at the local church and that is where we should look for her now. So on we go. We get to the church and Lorni spots our friend in a small side chapel. She skips inside joyfully, with Velu peering through the pillars to have a better view of what is happening. I choose to stay in the car. Lorni returns overjoyed. We have found our friend at last! Velu is also full of smiles as we get back into the car on our homeward journey. As we cannot speak to our friend now, Lorni has arranged to meet her the following week.

"Good thing no lady that we found that missi. But hopeless place this is lady, nobody knows any number and they don't know anything. Must tell that lady to stay somewhere else."

Velu is expounding on our afternoon's adventure.

Lorni is very pleased. "I never give up," she says proudly.

As we wend our way homewards, I cannot help but wonder where 694 was anyway - did it really exist or was it some figment of our imagination? And where oh where were the white flags?

The Lesson

I could hardly believe my eyes – it was Kolitha waving to me from across the room. Why, I hadn't seen him for maybe five years! We had first met at the small restaurant near our workplaces. At that time we felt we were aliens from outer space. That's what the US seemed to us – two simple unsophisticated people who had to get used to this incredibly ordered way of life, where systems worked and we ourselves had to work very hard. Hardly any holidays - unlike at home where there were Saturdays and Sundays and Poya days and weekends which we made longer by cutting work on the Monday or the Friday. But here, in America, we had to work and work and work. Leisure time was hard to come by and had to be earned.

I'll never forget the day Kolitha and I met. I went over to the snack joint near the office - Sonny's Place, for my usual after-work drink and dinner- it was easier than having to cook at home.

As I ordered my gin and tonic, the barman, a friendly Jamaican leaned over.

"Over there," he pointed with his chin, "I think that guy is from your country."

Sipping my drink I turned around. He was sitting alone at a small table in the far corner, peering into the menu. All I could see was a bald head, two sticking out ears, hands folded on the table. I walked up to him, and as I approached I coughed deliberately. He looked up with a start. His oversized glasses kept falling off his nose.

"Hi – I'm Gihan de Silva."

"Oh – hello,' he blurted, "I'm Ko."

"Ko – that's an unusual name – or is it ko for where?" I laughed.

"No no – I'm Kolitha Imbuldeniya – but here I'm calling myself Ko Imbul – much easier no. You know these Americans no, they can't pronounce anything."

I smiled. We chatted and soon we were sharing a table. I ordered my favourite steak and hash browns, piled over with carrots, green peas and sliced tomatoes.

I couldn't help notice that Ko had ordered a very frugal meal – in fact it was just a plate of fries and tomato sauce. I knew that the sauce came free with the fries. He poured the sauce onto his plate and dipped each fry into it coating it carefully on all sides before he put it into his mouth.

Maybe he wasn't hungry – or didn't like the food here.

The next day he was there again. And the next, and the next. His diet was the always the same.

"Hey Ko, " I said, "Don't you eat anything else?"

"No machang – early morning I eat some bread and beef curry. For lunch I eat two sandwiches and this is my dinner. Otherwise it becomes too expensive – who can spend so much on food, when I have to save money for the rains. On the weekends I eat a big plate of rice and curry for lunch – nothing else, because everything is so expensive."

I felt a pang of guilt as I savoured my succulent chicken baked in cheese sauce. My god, I must have spent a fortune on food, such waste - what a lot I could have saved!

Ko must've seen the look on my face. He shook his head. "That's what – now see, you waste so much money on all these expensive dishes – and you must be spending so much on clothes also." He eyed my designer shirt and tie with disapproval.

I began to think about Ko and his saving ways. A twinge of guilt crept over me whenever we met, as his 'saving' ways seemed to point a long hard finger of disapproval at me. Gradually these twinges intensified and even when I was alone I would think of what a spendthrift I was. I would gaze around my room and tick off in my mind all the unnecessary expensive items that were scattered around. We were both in the same category of work – way down in the computer line and I spent most of my salary on food, and clothes and generally having a good time. I could imagine Ko having a nice fat wad of money stashed away safely – for the rains, as he described it. I pictured myself in a few years, old and panting, still running in the same place with not a cent saved.

After work I went as usual to Sonny's armed with a sense of determination and with Ko's help I tried to eat less – not less in quantity but less in cost. Ko did the ordering for me – there never seemed to be anything cheaper than chips, or even better, popcorn which was free. But I was hungry all the time, especially as I never had a proper breakfast. At work my stomach rumbled in protest and I had to sneak in some sandwiches and hamburgers to pacify it.

The next time we met I dared to ask. "Hey Ko – where can I get some cheap clothes?"

"Ah – I go to a warehouse a few miles from here – you can get things really cheap – I'll take you if you want."

So the next Saturday we made a trip together to the S & M. Warehouse. I was stunned by the expanse of the building and even more surprised at the low prices. But much to my chagrin, nothing really took my fancy and what ever little did, didn't fit me. Shirts, pants, shoes – they were all the same – either too small or too big. I cursed at my bad luck. Here was I trying seriously to save some dollars and all my efforts proved futile.

"This shirt is only one size too big – it's so cheap you should buy it," Ko was placing a shirt against my shoulders.

So I bought it. After all what was one size too big? He made me wear a pair of shoes, a size too small. My feet pinched.

"What is one size machang, they will stretch in no time. When you go home stuff it with newspaper and that will make them stretch.

So when I got home I tore up some paper and made them into balls to stuff my shoes. They looked quite funny bulging as though they were about to burst.

I wore them both to work the next day. By midday I felt as though my toes were being put through a mincing machine, but I reckoned by the end of the day things would work out. What really happened was quite different. I had to teeter around the office as I could hardly put my feet down flat. In addition my rolled up shirt sleeves which hung down my arms made me the butt end of my colleagues' weird sense of humour.

"I say, what's this – decided to become an angel? Tippy toeing along with your sleeves flapping!"

"Are you planning to put on weight or what?" my Sri Lankan friends teased.

I cursed that I had ever fallen for Ko's persuasive talk. Such damn nonsense, I thought, as I threw my shirt and the shoes under my bed when I got home. What a damn waste of money, I thought.

My foolishness dawned on me like one of those strange revelations one reads about. Why the hell was I trying to be like Ko in the first place - to save money for the rains, as he said? Well now I cared a damn hoot whether it rained or poured – I decided to revert to my old comfortable lifestyle.

As usual, I saw him the next day at Sonny's Place. There he was, seated at the corner table, drinking a glass of water. The miser, I snarled to myself. Look at him, his head minus most of its hair – maybe he was saving that somewhere too; his shirt a size too small making him all hunched up. He was picking at his usual chips and tomato sauce. He looked like an outsized insect picking at remnants.

I'm definitely not going to sit with him. Avoid him like an infectious disease, I told myself. He was worse than it. I didn't want to catch the 'saving' sickness again. I spent as I always did, and concentrated on my work. In a few months I got a promotion. My work took on more responsibility. I worked late often and didn't have the time to go for my after-work drink at Sonny's Place. Within months I changed my workplace to another part of the city – a better job and a more comfortable life was my reward for all the hard work I'd done over the past few years. I had lost touch with Ko, although I did think of him from time to time, especially when I ate chips and tomato sauce. I wondered how his savings for the rains were getting on.

And now there he was, right across the room waving his hand vigorously to me. My first reaction was to ignore him. Pretend you haven't seen him, a little voice whispered, just walk the other way. But the years had mellowed my feelings towards him. It was so long ago that now it seemed to be quite funny when I thought about it. In fact a sudden wave of nostalgia swept over me, as I moved across the room to greet him.

"Hi Ko – good to see you man, after what - almost five years no? So how are you?" I shook his hand firmly.

I noticed a young woman by his side. She looked up shyly as he introduced us.

"Ah Leesha – meet my old friend Gihan- we used to meet after work almost every day long years ago. Gihan this is my wife Leesha."

He took me aside, "Managed to get a good catch from Sri Lanka machang, " he nudged my elbow and rolled his eyes, "good dowry also -house and money here and there also." He squeezed my arm making me squirm. He was now completely bald. While I had put on some weight he remained the same thin scrawny fellow he used to be. Leesha was small made and had dark twinkling eyes and a smile that lit up her delicate elfin face. How the hell did he get such a good catch, I asked myself. I wish I had the luck to meet someone like that!

He gave me his business card and I realized he too had moved to another part of the city. I noted he lived in a popular residential area and was impressed to see that he was the CEO of a computer firm. "My own business," he said proudly.

I gazed at him in wonder. My goodness, I thought, he certainly had made the best of things, So now he had his savings plus a fat dowry to see him through the rains. Maybe he had changed his miserly ways, after all, it was a long time since we'd met. Trying to act unconcerned, I gave him my card as well, feeling proud of my own achievement as Senior Supervisor of the most prestigious Computer Software company in the region. He must've changed, I thought, as we chatted and walked through the shop.

Leesha picked up a blouse, but Ko had one look at the price tag and said, "Far too much – we'll wait for the sales and try to get something cheap."

"But Ko – I really like this one and haven't bought anything for so many months." He held her elbow and egged her forward.

My god! He hasn't changed one bit, I reckoned. He's still the same stingy fool I knew. I followed them within earshot just to prove myself right, or hopefully, wrong.

After doing this for almost half an hour even I was becoming frustrated just seeing them walking around picking up things and then putting them back. The fool Ko – how could he do this to his wife? At least he could be generous to her. The poor girl, I could see her picking up the odd blouse or skirt and gaze at them with glistening eyes, only to be told over and over again that it cost too much! Looking at them across the room I wondered whether he had put her also on the chips and tomato sauce diet – they both looked thin – almost half starved. I gasped. I saw her dragging herself along, hands hanging limply by her side, her face wearing a distinct look of dejection. And there was Ko- scrawny, bald headed, huge glasses falling off his nose, stick hands and claw fingers. A real monster. Suddenly an idea flashed across my mind. I would treat them to lunch and give her the best meal she'd ever had – that'll teach him a good lesson! I hurried towards them and tapped Ko on his back.

"I say – how about I stand both of you lunch – after all we haven't met for so many years."

Ko looked nervous. But Leesha beamed, her eyes almost popping out of her head. She gave a little clap - "Oh - we'll love that – won't we Kolitha?"

Soon we were seated at a trendy restaurant nearby. The waiter hovered over us.

"Anything to drink?" he inquired.

"Just water for us," said Ko hurriedly, pointing to his wife and himself.

"Would you like some wine?"

"Oh I'd love that." Leesha's voice had a distinct lilt in it.

"Oh no – wine's too expensive. We never drink wine -" Ko looked sharply at her as if she had misbehaved in public.

"No – no have some, after all this is a celebration – ha ha." I said, waving my hand "Red or white?"

"I don't know – I've never had any – but I'd like to try -" She shrugged.

"It's too much – " Ko butted in.

Ignoring him, I consulted with the waiter and settled for a bottle of white wine.

"Have some – I'm sure you'll like it."

She just smiled.

We studied the Menu cards while we waited.

Ko was fidgeting with the card. First he looked on one side, the other, and then back again. He drummed his fingers on the table.

Leesha studied the Menu painstakingly, almost savouring all the ingredients listed there.

"Do you like seafood?" I asked her.

"Yes – oh yes – but-" looking at Ko, knowing she was being rash in her statements now.

"It's ridiculous – the prices here. There's a much cheaper place just across the street-"

"That's okay Ko – this is on me –" I looked across at Leesha – "Order whatever you like."

"Oh so many things I don't know what to choose." Her voice could hardly be heard. After a while she said "I'll have the grilled prawns and Caesar salad."

"Have a soup," I said. "Try the French onion – it's good. I'm having the salmon with mushroom sauce. Hey -try a starter – the avocado in lemon cream is excellent."

The wine had come by now. "Cheers – and all the best." We clinked glasses- at least Leesha and I did. Ko sat there sipping his water, looking at the wine like it was poison.

So we gorged our way through soups, starters, salads, wine and more wine, and by the time we had reached the main course stage, Leesha had become very talkative. Ko sat silently nibbling his Chicken Wings in Soy sauce.

"Would you like some caviar Sir," the waiter gave us a wide smile.

I looked at Leesha and raised my eyebrows, when she smiled, her cheeks dimpling, I knew it was okay.

"Yes yes – bring on some caviar and another bottle of wine."

Leesha was laughing a lot now and telling me all about how she met Ko and got married and about her job here. The wine was going down pretty fast between the two of us. Ko just stuck to his water and glowered at his wife and me.

The desserts were delectable, Chocolate Mousse, Lemon Meringue – but again Ko chose the cheapest item on the menu. "I'll just have ice cream, one scoop," he said to the waiter who was amused because here they never served anything less than three scoops – topped with something or another. Leesha started to giggle and I grinned silently, my insides just bursting.

"Coffee or tea?" the waiter looked around at us.

"Irish coffee for me," I said.

Leesha looked non plussed.

"Hey Ko – how about an Irish Coffee?"

He peered at the Menu. "Madness- it's far too much, I'll just have a tea."

"Come on Leesha – have something special – how about a Cappuccino?"

"Alright, alright, anything you say, I'll have," she twittered.

The whole drama enacted in making the Irish Coffee held her spellbound.

I felt good inside. Especially when I looked at the two of them. Leesha looked thoroughly ecstatic – she'd really gone to town. Perhaps her best meal since she landed in this country. Ko looked like he was about to collapse.

I flicked my fingers at the waiter to bring the bill.

When it came I went through it in detail. My goodness we had had a real treat! The bill was colossal! I'll show the fool, I thought as I pulled out my wallet and passed on my Visa card. The waiter took the bill away and returned a few minutes later. He bent towards my ear.

"Sir," he whispered, "we don't accept Visa."

"What?"

"Yes – only American Express, sorry Sir."

"But I don't have American Express- hey – can't you check with the Manager? What's wrong with Visa?"

"Nothing sir. Just that we accept only American Express sir."

"But this is ridiculous! What happens if I don't have American Express? Ha – then what?"

Our lowered tones had certainly gone up by a few decibels by now, and I could feel several eyes on us.

The waiter looked hard at me. Then he bent down again and I could feel his hot breath in my ear. "Why then – then, it'll have to be cash sir."

Cash, cash – the mere word made me freeze. Here was I, proud owner of a credit card, never carrying too much cash on me, now being asked for cash to pay this – this massive, gigantic, gargantuan bill? What the hell was I to do? I fumbled with sweaty fingers as I peered into my wallet. Some dollar bills and small change looked bleakly at me. Glancing through them I realized I had just enough to pay the waiter a tip.

The waiter stood by, rocking on his heels, gawking over my head, like a predatory bird about to devour its prey.

The deathly silence at the table was pressing down on me I could hardly breathe. What was I to do? Of course I could go to the bank and take out some cash but I needed the money now – this very second.

Sensing my great discomfiture Leesha spoke – "What's the matter?"

"It's just, just, - they don't accept Visa and I don't have enough cash."

"Oh that's okay, we can sort it out." Leesha patted my hand.

I looked up, first at Leesha whose eyes were fixed on Ko, and then at Ko himself. whose eyes were bulging like two black stones out of his paan piti face.

"Don't worry Gihan – Kolitha can easily pay, can't you Kolitha?" Leesha's voice seemed to ring out from somewhere far away. She held her hand over her mouth and giggled.

In a haze I saw the bill float in the waiter's hand, take an arc over my head , and land in front of Ko.

I swallowed hard. I mustn't lose control of myself, not before Ko anyway. I cleared my throat - "Hey Ko, thanks very much machang – sorry about this. Okay then that's settled. Here take this for the tip." Passing him some notes I got up quickly in case he changed his mind.

I glanced at my watch. "Goodness I'm already late for a meeting in office. Must run." I stood up and leaned over to Leesha. "Lovely meeting you Leesha, and Ko – it's super seeing you again."

But Ko didn't reply. He was examining the bill, as the waiter leaned over his shoulder.

Leesha placed her elbows on the table and cupped her face in her hands. "So lovely to meet you Gihan," she held my hand briefly, squeezing it ever so gently. " Do keep in touch - hope we see you again- soon." Her eyes had an unmistakable twinkle in them as she spoke.